Titles by *Langaa* RPCIG

Francis B. Nyamnjoh
Stories from Abakwa
Mind Searching
The Disillusioned African
The Convert
Souls Forgotten
Married But Available

Dibussi Tande
No Turning Back. Poems of Freedom 1990-1993
Scribbles from the Den: Essays on Politics and Collective
Memory in Cameroon

Kangsen Feka Wakai
Fragmented Melodies

Ntemfac Ofege
Namondo, Child of the Water Spirits
Hot Water for the Famous Seven

Emmanuel Fru Doh
Not Yet Damascus
The Fire Within
Africa's Political Wastelands: The Bastardization of
Cameroon
Oriki'badan
Wading the Tide

Thomas Jing
Tale of an African Woman

Peter Wuteh Vakunta
Grassfields Stories from Cameroon
Green Rape: Poetry for the Environment
Majunga Tok: Poems in Pidgin English
Cry, My Beloved Africa
No Love Lost
Straddling The Mungo: A Book of Poems in English &
French

Ba'bila Mutia
Coils of Mortal Flesh

Kehbuma Langmia
Titabet and the Takumbeng
An Evil Meal of Evil

Victor Elame Musinga
The Barn
The Tragedy of Mr. No Balance

Ngessimo Mathe Mutaka
Building Capacity: Using TEFL and African Languages as
Development-oriented Literacy Tools

Milton Krieger
Cameroon's Social Democratic Front: Its History and
Prospects as an Opposition Political Party, 1990-2011

Sammy Oke Akombi
The Raped Amulet
The Woman Who Ate Python
Beware the Drives: Book of Verse

Susan Nkwentie Nde
Precipice
Second Engagement

**Francis B. Nyamnjoh &
Richard Fonteh Akum**
The Cameroon GCE Crisis: A Test of Anglophone
Solidarity

Joyce Ashuntantang & Dibussi Tande
Their Champagne Party Will End! Poems in Honor of
Bate Besong

Emmanuel Achu
Disturbing the Peace

Rosemary Ekosso
The House of Falling Women

Peterkins Manyong
God the Politician

George Ngwane
The Power in the Writer: Collected Essays on Culture,
Democracy & Development in Africa

John Percival
The 1961 Cameroon Plebiscite: Choice or Betrayal

Albert Azeyeh
Réussite scolaire, faillite sociale : généalogie mentale de
la crise de l'Afrique noire francophone

Aloysius Ajab Amin & Jean-Luc Dubois
Croissance et développement au Cameroun :
d'une croissance équilibrée à un développement équitable

Carlson Anyangwe
Imperialistic Politics in Cameroun:
Resistance & the Inception of the Restoration of the
Statehood of Southern Cameroons

Bill F. Ndi
K'Cracy, Trees in the Storm and Other Poems
Map: Musings On Ars Poetica
Thomas Lurting: The Fighting Sailor Turn'd Peaceable /
Le marin combattant devenu paisible

**Kathryn Toure, Therese Mungah
Shalo Tchombe & Thierry Karsenti**
ICT and Changing Mindsets in Education

Charles Alobwed'Epie
The Day God Blinked

G.D. Nyamndi
Babi Yar Symphony
Whether losing, Whether winning
Tussles: Collected Plays

Samuel Ebelle Kingue
Si Dieu était tout un chacun de nous?

Ignasio Malizani Jimu
Urban Appropriation and Transformation : bicycle, taxi
and handcart operators in Mzuzu, Malawi

Justice Nyo' Wakai:
Under the Broken Scale of Justice: The Law and My
Times

John Eyong Mengot
A Pact of Ages

Ignasio Malizani Jimu
Urban Appropriation and Transformation: Bicycle Taxi
and Handcart Operators

Joyce B. Ashuntantang
Landscaping and Coloniality: The Dissemination of
Cameroon Anglophone Literature

Jude Fokwang
Mediating Legitimacy: Chieftaincy and Democratisation in
Two African Chiefdoms

Michael A. Yanou
Dispossession and Access to Land in South Africa: an
African Perspevctive

Tikum Mbah Azonga
Cup Man and Other Stories

Imitation Whiteman

Vivian Sihshu Yenika

Langaa Research & Publishing CIG
Mankon, Bamenda

Publisher:
Langaa RPCIG
Langaa Research & Publishing Common Initiative Group
P.O. Box 902 Mankon
Bamenda
North West Region
Cameroon
Langaagrp@gmail.com
www.langaa-rpcig.net

Distributed outside N. America by African Books Collective
orders@africanbookscollective.com
www.africanbookscollective.com

Distributed in N. America by Michigan State University
Press
msupress@msu.edu
www.msupress.msu.edu

ISBN: 9956-558-80-X

DISCLAIMER

The names, characters, places and incidents in this book are either the product of the author's imagination or are used fictitiously. Accordingly, any resemblance to actual persons, living or dead, events, or locales is entirely one of incredible coincidence.

Other books by the same Author

Contents

Dedication

For those with the courage to do the right thing!

Part One

Chapter One

The truck was already pulling away when Martin Tebi quickly signed his name on what looked like a *scrap* of paper and hurried toward it. There was room enough for his left foot as he struggled to board the overcrowded truck squeezing through the numerous bodies that stood above him. The man at the office down the street had said they were going far, far away south to start working with a new company that had just moved into the area. He could tell his fellow passengers were as excited as he was. *Who* was not? They were whispering excitedly about the prospects of a better life with this new white man's company. For a minute, he envisioned his life as it would be from then on. He saw himself riding a brand new motorcycle on a deserted street, hooting at young, pretty women just waiting there for the "Big man." It all seemed so real and felt so good. What else could it be? The man in the office had also remarked that he was one of the five literate men they had recruited that week. The hiring staff had mentioned this with a big grin on his face. It could only mean one thing: Martin was going to be a Big man in this place where the white people were trying to open some kind of factory. He would have to choose between working in one of the offices or in the fields, so the recruiter had said. But in Martin's heart there was only one choice, and that was the office; any job that included pen and paper and, which kept him far away from the palm fields where he heard were heavily infested with snakes, mosquitoes and strange bugs. Just thinking about the possibility of having a job outdoors on one of the plantation fields gave him the chills. He was a grass field man and did not want to encounter any of those

3

strange bugs that crawled all over the thick bushes in that part of the country. There should be a better alternative to the fields. No, no, no; he did not want a job working in the fields at all!

The truck was *pushing* its way up the station hill as its passengers swayed from one side to another unperturbed. They were shouting and singing; some even clapping their hands to show how happy they were with their decision to venture out to this unknown land in search of some kind of fortune. They were healthy young men in their late teens and early twenties who otherwise would have been stranded in the village somewhere with no other choice but to work on the farm for nothing. They were quite excited and grateful for this rare opportunity to better their lives. At least, their fate would be different or so they thought. They were no longer trapped in a life of endless labour on tiny farms that yielded very little. Yes, the farms had served their parents well; none of them could disagree with this. However, it was these same farms that had also broken their parents' youthful bodies inch by inch adding unnecessary wrinkles onto their faces and forcing them into early graves. These same farms had begun mangling their strong bodies too. The first year of intense labour cost one a toe or two; the next year would be something else and so on. What a relief to finally find an alternative to such a predictable lifestyle of hard labour! They did have a choice after all, unlike their fathers who had continued with the farming tradition of their forefathers. For once, they would be earning money working on a farm owned by a stranger! They would be earning salaries like some of the few literate people they knew about right there in Bamenda, and others they had heard about who had become Big men in the coastal regions of the country.

The truck made a sharp turn and they all swayed to one side again screaming and totally thrilled with the experience. It felt like an adventure they had been waiting for all their lives; only this was being financed by someone they did not even know and had never met. In fact, they knew very little about the colonial company they were heading down south to work for. But no one cared. Martin finally got both of his feet down on the floor of the truck and left his body to be shoved to whatever direction the truck went. So far, he was enjoying the ride too and was also fascinated by the enthusiasm of the other recruits who were heading to the same destination — he imagined. He tried counting the heads in the truck but just couldn't. There were too many black heads in there; no bald heads or heads with gray hair. And two thirds of these passengers had no shirts on. He could not see their feet but he imagined they had no shoes on as well. They seemed like a pathetic bunch of people with torn khaki shorts covering their half naked bodies, and they all stank like hell from the sweat that oozed from every part of their bodies. Some even had brown armpits with stinking water freely gliding down their rib cages. Martin did not bother about this. He could spot two other people there who were properly clothed like him in clean shirts and khaki trousers. Every so often their heads would surface and their hands would cling tightly to the rails of the truck. One had a tear under the left armpit of his otherwise clean cotton shirt. Martin suspected they were the literate ones. He could catch a glimpse of a smile on one of the faces every now and then. But occasionally, he also saw doubt or what he interpreted as fear in their eyes, and would notice one making a sign of the cross. Ah! He let out a gasp. Indeed, that one was not sure, he noted in his mind and continued watching these passengers who from all indication exuded promise. Another stared at the hand holding on to the rails and murmured something Martin was unable to decipher. He grinned. From their actions he could sense exactly how they felt. Had they all not embarked on the trip to the coast, a place where none of them had ever visited or could ever imagine how people lived to search for something better? But what lay ahead no one knew. All they had heard was that the Europeans had opened a big plantation down south and that there were lots of job opportunities for those able, strong and willing to put in long hours. Martin sighed as he brushed his chin on his limp shirt collar. Was he able and strong? He wondered. Perhaps so, he nodded and grinned looking across the overcrowded truck at some of his fellow passengers again. Their eyes shifted from side to side squinting at the edges as each strained to make out the town they had just passed or the people they had just seen hawking food by the road side. Some eyes would brighten up as passengers thought they recognized someone on the street they had just driven by or through; or something – anything and a smile would creep on their lips but not for long, for the truck drove past quickly before they could finish savouring the moment. This happened repeatedly and soon more passengers began whispering prayers and making signs of the cross before shifting their eyes elsewhere in search of something familiar. Anything that would assure them that all would be fine, the eyes searched. Martin's eyes darted from side to side too; but he was a strong man who would not show fear. Neither would he show anxiety by praying like the others. Why should he really? He thought. After all, he was not the only one in that vehicle heading to a strange town to work for some strange people. So why should he doubt his decision?

In an era when few people could read and write he was one of the privileged few. All the twenty standard six graduates of his father's generation held very important posts in the government. They were either Secretaries of States or government Ministers. West Cameroon needed literate people so badly that the government officials had begun recruiting even standard one dropout as clerks all over the place. Now was Martin's turn. He actually had his standard six Certificate locked up in his suitcase back at Nkwen. He did not want to travel with it. The Big man at the recruiting office had never bothered to see his credentials. He simply said, "your name?"

"My name is Martin Tebi, sir."

"How old are you?"

"I am twenty-years old, sir."

Then he had smiled and begun chewing on the tip of his ball-point pen.

"Do you like money?" He had asked suddenly scribbling, down something next to Martin's name on his list.

"Yes, sir."

It was at that point that he had shaken Martin's hand and had given him a paper to sign. He told him that good life was indeed waiting for him in this new place where he was going. But the place was very, very far, he had cautioned him. Martin could tell however, that the man was not a fool. Eventually, they would want to see his certificate, to verify his credentials.

The truck driver stopped at a police check-point and gave the three policemen guarding the post some money. Martin knew it was money that had exchanged hands; what else could the driver be offering them wrapped in a sheet of paper? He also thought it would be odd for any officer of the law to let a truck load of almost a hundred men to just drive through like that! They wouldn't be doing their duty as law enforcement officers. As the truck trudged on to the unknown, the men began to sing. It was a very long and winding road but they kept their inharmonious melody going forever, taking turns to sleep while standing in the belly of the truck. By the time they arrived in Loum, a border town that separated English-speaking and French-speaking Cameroon they were already tired of the music as they watched dusk set in. The driver made one stop to feed his hungry stomach and empty his bladder. He was about to get into the truck and take off again without a care when Martin shouted – in spite of himself – "What about us, na driver?"

The driver stopped the engine.

"Eh?" He barked impatiently at the voice not caring to see who had spoken.

"We are hungry too, and we want to urinate too," Martin added defiantly.

The driver came out of the truck and attempted a head count of his cargo but could not. He shrugged his shoulders and was about to go back to his seat and continue the journey when the men burst out chanting: "Chop, chop," in a monosyllabic tone.

"Alright." He went to a store and got a basket of scones, which he carefully handed over to Martin leaning dangerously close to the back rail to distribute among the others. As the driver made for his seat again, he told them to urinate from up there. At first, they did not get what he meant then one passenger began laughing, tugging his friend by the ribs.

"We are cows and goats now." They laughed even harder.

The driver screamed back at them.

"Wuna be NEW Recruits!"

At this he took off at a deadly speed. There was no way he was going to let them out to urinate. What for? As it got darker the men took the driver's advice and one by one they leaned over and urinated over the railings. It was a strange sight. Martin remarked that the difference between them and cows was that they could empty their bladders on the street as opposed to just letting urine flow down in the truck, and making the metal bed more slippery than it already was.

Soon they entered a new town. The driver honked three times to alert them that they were quite close.

"*Na Kumba dis-oh, New Recruits!*"

"Yeah-eh!" They cheered not knowing the difference

8

since it was extremely dark with the streets abandoned. But they could see some dotted lights at a great distance. The truck stepped on something and bounced hard then jerked from side to side as the driver struggled to gain control of the vehicle. It bounced again and finally balanced on all four tires but nothing bad happened. The truck driver pushed forward until the dotted lamps disappeared. The vehicle like its passengers moaned from extreme fatigue as it performed its duty hauling these people to the land of Hope. Behind, the people had stopped talking and singing with many dozing and others humming under their breath to keep their spirits high. They drove miles and miles again hours on end bouncing on objects they could not see and listening to the driver cursing each time this happened. Finally, he announced: *"Na Lobe dis-oh!"* Martin could sense some form of relief in the man's voice. No one bothered to respond from behind. The driver plunged into a path that seemed to be heading into the thicket of a forest. He announced again: *"Na Lobe dis-oh, New Recruits!"* Martin suspected that they had finally arrived at their destination, Lobe Estate!

All the men remained quiet. Martin sighed and for the first time since he had signed that paper some twenty hours ago he felt disappointed and almost panicked. What had he traded Bamenda for? A strange calm overtook the truck. Nobody could utter a word, for none could tell what awaited them yet in this wilderness they were heading to, and that would eventually become their home as employees on this colonial plantation. This was the moment the driver loved the most. He began whistling an unfamiliar tune and when nobody challenged him, he coughed. *"Ah say, they don tie wuna tongue up there?"*

No one bothered to reply.

"What has happened to your tongues, na?" He repeated in English. Still they ignored him.

"You want work, you get work. Wetin you want again?" He went on as the truck galloped from one pothole to another. Slowly, he descended a hill. *"New Recruits, na African Hill dis-oh!"*

His voice drummed loud into their ears once again as they drove past the last village that separated the colonial property from other lands. They could see dim lights from what seemed like a cluster of huts alongside the road. The passengers listened to the engine grinding its way up and down what they conjectured was a windy road, watching the lights fade away gradually as they headed further down the road. The truck rose from a valley and its head lights landed on tall palm trees neatly arranged in rows. Next, the lights blared onto a bill board. Martin craned to read the words on the bill board but could only succeed in reading the last part from the flickers of the headlights before the lights drifted elsewhere. 'PALM ESTATE,' he read to himself and wondered what exactly was waiting for him on such an estate.

One last turn and Martin could spot a series of lights from afar. They looked different from the one that came from the headlights. But before he could exhale the men had begun whispering among themselves excitedly.

"New Recruits, na Lobe dis-oh! Law beh," he repeated dragging out the two syllables deliberately so the recruits would understand how their new home is called. The recruits burst into singing again. Martin brought a kola nut from his pocket and managed to squeeze a lobe into his mouth. He chewed vigorously and watched the truck wheel to a stop in front of a building. The florescent lights shone into their eyes blinding them as they shouted with joy. Martin could see the driver standing by the vehicle and waiting for them to jump off. He too was now peeling and tossing lobes of kola nuts into his mouth. He saw the man wipe his forehead with a towel before shutting his door. The new recruits got out of the truck pausing to stretch their legs and waists as they awaited further instructions. Martin could see the driver

returning from an office with a bag of garri and a big ledger. He wondered. The driver waved the bag in front of them and announced: *"Your chop for morning."* They were glad to hear that they would be having something for breakfast; better yet, something familiar. They clapped and hopped back onto the truck for him to take them to their place of rest, which was only half a block away.

As they slept that night on mattresses in their carefully chosen groups of ten or so, Martin smiled. Silently, he thought about the ordeal and convinced himself that it was going to be alright after all. They were actually sleeping on Dunlop mattresses! That was something, he conceded. It was a very short night for all of them though. He couldn't help overhearing the other recruits whispering under the calico sheet they were given to use as blankets. Some said it was too hot; yes, he nodded in his quiet corner, and there were lots of mosquitoes. But their mattresses were so comfortable it was hard to feel the other discomforts. Martin agreed with his fellow recruits. He took one last look at their new surroundings, gazing through the piles of tired bodies that sprawled on the floor until his eyes landed on this one man. At first, he could not figure out what he was busy doing. However, as he concentrated harder he realized that the man was scratching his name on his calico blanket. He followed the man's hand gesture reading each letter as the man scrawled it in black ink right in the middle of the blanket: PUIS. Martin chuckled as he watched the man grin with satisfaction.

"What?" The man asked.

"Nothing."

Chapter Two

The next morning all the men who could not read and write were taken to the fields where they were told what was expected of them by one stout black man wearing a metal military cap on his head. He explained later to them that it was an "iron cap" he had inherited from his European boss. The boss had told him he would make a fine leader some day. The iron cap man smiled showing a few white teeth. Martin was impressed. The man cleared his throat and frowned. The new recruits stood up straight. He relaxed and said it was his duty to show the new recruits around before the white manager could set eyes on them. They were to be at their best behaviour when that time came. This stout black man took all 98 of them to a large store in the huge factory and gave each a pair of clothing and rubber boots to dress up for the occasion. He warned them that the white man liked hardworking people, so they should work hard to impress him. And if they wanted a smile from him, they should look clean at all times no matter what! Even if they had just retrieved palm bunches from a mud puddle. Also, it was their jobs as harvesters to be efficient and respectful, and to obey orders from above. There would be no exceptions to this rule.

As he expected, Martin was taken to another office to meet a Big man. There, they introduced him to a Big man sitting in a rolling chair. The office boy said the man was the office supervisor – the only black man in the young company with such a rank. This Big man did not bother to look up as the messenger pushed the new recruit inside the tiny office. The edges of his crisp, starched white short-sleeve shirt pointed to the sides as the man struggled to

13

adjust his buttocks onto his seat. He looked too big for his shirt which had a missing button in the middle. The man's eyes were glued to a pile of papers on his small wooden table, on which he traced his name and title repeatedly, pausing to admire each tracing every now and again. He tore and tossed aside those he did not like and finally held one in the air toward the day light with a grin of satisfaction. He then leaned over to put the sheet of paper away.

Martin stood still and waited. He had been standing there unnoticed for a couple of minutes so he decided to say something. He cleared his throat and said: "good morning, sir."

"Morning" was the curt reply he received. Martin waited. The man opened his drawer, pulled out an exercise book, flipped through it and returned it where it belonged. He pulled open a second drawer and got out a purple ledger, flipped through this and positioned it on the desk. He sighed and picked up the ledger again. Martin remained standing there; his legs were getting sore. He looked around the room and saw four empty chairs waiting. The man noticed his eyes wandering around his room.

"What is it, young fellow? Can't you stand on your feet one minute?"

"Yes, sir. I can stand, sir."

"Good, because you see, we don't like lazy men here. Palm-oil is not made by lazy people."

"Yes, sir," Martin replied sheepishly and stood erect once more. The man continued to fidget with the pages of the big book that lay in front of him. The door opened slightly behind Martin and in a flash the man hurried out of the room. Minutes later, he returned with a stack of letters for the messenger.

"Where were we, young fellow?" he asked.

"I was here just waiting, sir."

"Oh, yes. Now I remember. Since you have been such a good boy, I will give you a chance to choose the kind of job

14

you want to do in our company, eh?" He looked up at Martin.

"Yes, sir."

"Hospital or field?" He presented the options clasping his hands behind his head and twirling on the rolling office chair. Martin noticed the armpits of the man's shirt. They looked kind of yellowish contrasting with the white front. He could see the man's white singlet through the unbuttoned portion of the shirt. Martin was impressed. So the man did wear singlets like those Europeans? Amazing.

The Big man waited.

"Young fellow?"

"Oh, sir, anything you give me is fine."

The man leaned forward, placing his elbows on the desk. "See, I'll be frank with you. If you want to be a Big man, go to the field. You know we are not many in this company. You and I are a special case. You can read and write like me, *no bi so?*" He eyed at him intensely and repeated the question, "not so?"

"Yes, sir," Martin answered.

"Okay then, go to work at once lazy fellow." The Big man ordered, his demeanour changing without warning.

Martin took a deep breath as he stepped out of that room into the open air. He could see the other literate men in their group queuing up to report to duty. Another truck was being prepared to search for potential workers from somewhere. Martin burst out laughing. He could not believe that the huge company truck labelled 'Man Diesel' was going out again to bring back more recruits. It was parked by the entrance to the factory waiting as a new driver stood by it beckoning to the mechanics to hurry up. By his side, stood the driver who had brought over Martin and his crew the night before.

"Driver, good morning," Martin greeted.

The middle aged man raised his cap and smiled sheepishly, "Good morning, *sah.*"

With his hands in his side pockets Martin began walking away then stopped. He stared at the driver for a moment. What did he just call him? That instance, he knew he was a Big man already. In his short life, no one had ever referred to him as a "sir." He waited for the other "young fellows" at the security guard's booth that stood at the entrance to the factory. Soon they came out smiling contentedly with eyes dazzling with anticipation.

"Boh," Martin ventured as the first one approached the booth.

"Field or hospital?"

The young fellow smiled. "No; for me it was office or field. I chose office of course!"

Martin looked at him dumbfounded.

"Office?"

The other nodded.

"But why?"

The man smiled. "Isn't that obvious?"

Martin did not know how to respond. So he shrugged the question away.

"I chose the field. My name is Martin Tebi," Martin introduced himself extending his right hand for a handshake.

Instead of taking the hand, the other young fellow burst out laughing. "Why, Martin? You can read and write; why do you choose dirt? That's for illiterates!" His sarcasm touched Martin so much Martin began scratching his head. He scooped out thick grease from his scalp on his finger nails and wiped it off his trousers, then became embarrassed at his actions. Was that kind of behaviour allowed?

"My name is Zacharias Fru." The young fellow jumped in interrupting Martin's thoughts. "Massa, *office, is where you'll meet those white men, na? Ah, ah, boh!*" He nodded with conviction. "Indeed, the office is the place, my friend," he said again watching the contours on Martin's face. Martin seemed unsure. The furrows on his forehead deepened. He stood for a moment and decided to leave. Zacharias followed him.

16

"You don't think so?"

Martin continued to walk away.

"Wait a minute, na!" Zacharias seized him by the elbow but Martin pulled away sighing.

Zacharias watched him walk away whistling; when Martin was just a few meters away, the man keeled over laughing his lungs out, not caring anymore whether Martin approved of his choice of work or not. Tears had started trickling down his cheeks when he heard footsteps behind him and turned around.

"You again? I thought you did not like my company."

Martin sighed and stared at the man hard. Unsure, he turned around to leave again.

"Is that how you will be, my friend?" Zacharias convulsed into laughter again muttering words under his breath Martin could not make out. He was still gloating when three other young fellows joined them. One named John had opted to work on the field; a fourth, Puis had opted for the factory, and Isaac, the fifth chose the hospital. Martin listening to these men discussing their options excitedly could not help but smile as he remembered Puis desperately printing his name on the company blanket.

"Martin," he approached the man and introduced himself almost startling him.

"So?" Puis retorted.

"I just wanted to greet you," Martin began walking away.

Puis scratched his head and followed him. "You do know it is Puis, not so?"

Martin halted, not sure what the man was blabbing about.

"P U I S is how I spell my name." He added. "Special spelling if you must know."

Martin shrugged and joined the others with Puis only a meter or two behind.

As they walked off it became evident to him that they would be the future Big men of the company, if they each played their cards well. His thoughts wandered off to his interview earlier that day with the Black boss, and he had to admit that he might have blundered. The first test and Martin felt he had already failed. He sighed and listened to the different reasons each one gave for opting for whatever area to work. He had nothing to contribute to the discussion and felt like a failure. But John reminded him that all was not yet over. Wasn't it? Martin wondered but kept this thought to himself and waited to see what would really happen.

Chapter Three

It took Martin a week to get used to the routine of getting up at 5 in the morning to wait by the truck that took him and his batch of harvesters every day to the fields. The ritual was the same every morning: He took roll call; made sure they had enough *garri to soak in cold water* for lunch; and ordered a basin of *puff puff* or gateau to take along for their breakfast.

On arrival at Field one, he assigned the day's task and wandered off somewhere to rest his legs. Every so often he would then check on the workers with his ledger in hand not hesitating to cross out a harvester's name from the book for doing a sloppy job.

"You there," he would call out.

"Yes, sah."

"You missed a tree."

"Yes, sah," the harvester would answer and dutifully go back to attend to the palm tree. When this happened, Martin would beam and watch the harvester adjust his sickle to a wooden extension, hook the ripe bunch of fruits, and pull until it came tumbling down. With each attempt to get the bunch off the tree Martin beamed with pride. So these men were actually listening to him. He was proud of himself. Satisfied with the job, he would place a check mark against the harvester's name, and compliment him. And so Martin's field experience fell into a nice routine.

"Hey you there, where is today's water?" Martin would shout at the Water Boy in charge of his fields and the young fellow would come running with a pail of water on his head.

"Here, sah."

He would nod and take the cup of water being extended to him and drink.

"Why is the water so warm today?"

"Sah, it is the sun."

"Next time, let it be cold, you hear?"

"Yes, sah."

"Always sit in the shade to keep it cold, you hear?"

"Yes, sah."

With that, he would dismiss the boy and smile. He thought he had a good grip of the job at first since all his workers listened to him and carried out his instructions. Martin felt like a Big man and liked the feeling. But then field work became too predictable and he became bored with the monotony and with the outdoors. Even so, he managed to stay on a little bit longer.

He had been doing this job for five months when he finally decided he did not like it at all. A couple of times, he stepped on stray faeces and twice he had fallen into a stream when the rotten log of wood that served as a bridge had disintegrated underneath him. As the rains began falling the company's boots and umbrella did not help him much as he had to spend time searching for a comfortable dry spot to place his behind day in, day out. One day, he could no longer handle it and was about to give up when John advised him on what to do. The very next day after talking to his friend, Martin went to the hospital and complained of stomach ache and sore throat. He was given a day off, which he gladly took and retired to the two room house he had been assigned to. With this discovery he saw hope after all and an easy way of becoming a real Big man. Thereafter, once every month he got two days off and usually these were the rainiest days of the month. He used this strategy throughout the rainy season and was ready to combat the dry season. But his workers had seen through his scheme and had nicknamed him "Fear, Fear Head Man!"

From then on he was to be known as such. The harvesters would wait for him to retreat to his usual spot after rationing out their daily task, before they would begin humming the name in a song. At first, he pretended he did not know what they were singing about. But one day, when he confronted a harvester who had taken some minutes off to rest in the shades, the harvester blatantly called him a "Fear, Fear Head Man" to his face. Stunned, Martin did just what his friend John would have done. He tore out a piece of paper from his book and wrote a lengthy report of insubordination to the white authorities. He described in detail how poor this man had conducted himself in the fields. The very next day, the poor harvester was suspended without pay for a month.

This infuriated the rest of the gang but they did not react immediately. Martin thought he had everything under control, until one day when a bunch of palm fruits almost dropped on him. It was an experience he would remember for a very long time. On that fateful day, he was coercing the harvesters to wrap up for the evening, so they would not keep the driver waiting for too long. But for some reason a handful of harvesters took their time. As Martin approached one to hasten him out of the field another decided to harvest one last bunch. It came tumbling at full speed toward Martin's head. He skipped out of there in time and saved his life but in his attempt to steer clear of the big bunch, he landed in the midst of dried prickly palm fronds. After much pain, he managed to lift himself up from the ground and confronted the harvester in question. But to his dismay, the man denied having been aware that the headman was anywhere near his section of palm trees. Martin placed an asterisk next to the man's name and limped away. Before letting the harvesters board the truck, he warned them of the possibilities of accidents like the one he had almost experienced that day, and reminded them to be more vigilant. The men apologized and said it would never happen again. Martin smiled and brushed off some dirt from his knee high rubber boots before joining the driver on the passenger side of the truck. Before the driver could turn on the engine Martin heard chuckles from the back of the truck. His face dropped and he looked away as the driver suppressed a chuckle of his own right there next to him.

A couple of months later he had a similar experience in another section of the field. This time the bunch almost got him and fell right next to his feet. Although the harvester was quick to apologize and actually knelt down to ask for pardon, Martin was sceptical. The man apologized repeatedly. "Sah, ah go lick your boots, if you want."

Martin looked at him grovelling down there and wondered if there was any shred of sincerity behind those words.

"Stand up, Andrew; next time, I may make you to actually lick my boots; do you hear? Now get up. I forgive you." The harvester thanked him and rose from the ground. Martin was not sure what to make of these near misses. Were the harvesters trying to kill him? God forbid! Had he not been a kind boss? When he related the story to John, his friend advised him to find a way to appease the workers before things got out of hand Martin thought John was insane. Was he not the person in charge of Field one? Was he not the Big man there? So why should he let them change the rules, especially since the company handbook had clear guidelines on how little people like harvesters should conduct themselves in the fields. Martin dismissed John's suggestions. Instead, he gathered all fifty of his men for a meeting one bright Friday afternoon and identified the leader.

"James," he began. "You and your followers should listen carefully to what I am going to say."

The man called James spat on the ground not far away from Martin's feet.

"We no di hear grammar-oh, Mr. Head man."

Martin ignored. "Well, you go try. Yes, you will try to understand English whether you like it or not," he repeated. He gazed at the endless fields of palm trees. They seemed so peaceful and yet so ominous. He turned and faced the harvesters again.

"If na Oga himself, will you not try to hear what he is saying? Is English my country talk?"

At the mention of the white boss the harvesters stiffened and waited. Martin liked that. "I will say it again; when the white Big man speaks, do you not hear?"

James chuckled. "Oga himself no di report cutting bangas."

"Na true," the others concurred that the white boss never reported harvesters to anyone.

Martin smiled broadly. "You are his harvesters; I'm sure you already know that." He remembered something and smiled again.

"Of course, he is the boss. Why will he report you; and who will he report you to again? Na my work that!" It was Martin's turn to laugh; and laugh he did, so loud that his workers were surprised.

"Just in case you forget; yes, it is my job!" he laughed again.

"Oga sacks lazy workers."

"Like you?" One harvester grunted from the crowd. The crowd burst out laughing too. At that moment, James started humming a tune. Martin's batch of field hands joined:

Ho slacker, slacker don come
Who don come?
Ho slacker, slacker don come!

Before Martin could catch his breath the men had dropped their harvesting tools and were jumping on their feet to the rhythm of the tune as they referred to him as a "slacker who had just arrived." They performed this subversive ritual for a couple of minutes then James signalled them to gather their stuff and head for the palm trees.

"Wait, you all. Wait..." Martin called out desperately. "The meeting is not yet over until I say so. I am the 'Sah' here!" he mimicked how they addressed him.

The men went on with their tune not paying heed to his command. So he was the "sir," so what? They disappeared into their assigned rows of palm trees and finished their tasks for the day. It was only then that they returned to the post where Martin sat checking his record. They ignored him and waited. Not long after that, the truck pulled up and they all hopped onto it as usual, and from up there they watched with disdain as their enfeebled headman snuggled into the front seat next to the driver.

From that day on things were never the same in the fields. Martin was blindfolded and tied onto a tree several times by somebody. He could not report this insubordination because he had not seen the men's faces; neither had he heard their voices. One night as he was returning home from his friend's place someone threw a bundle of excreta at him. That did it. He did not know for sure who did it, but he suspected that it was one of his workers. He finally gave up despite John's pleas and went back to the office to see the Black supervisor for a new assignment.

"What is it now, young fellow?" the man asked impatiently.

"I want a different job," Martin stated simply.

The man gazed at him for a moment and laughed. "Factory or hospital?"

Martin started to say factory then he remembered Puis had mentioned a boiler incident. He could not remember the exact details, although he could still see the frightening expression on Puis' face as he related the story. Martin winced. Maybe the hospital. He weighed this option in his mind but then he also remembered Isaac saying the real nurses were too bossy. Perhaps office would be the best option, he thought. For a moment he pictured his friend Zacharias always running errands for all the senior staff. Zacharias had boasted that the white managers trusted him more than they did the older messenger. Martin pondered whether he truly wanted to be an errand boy, but decided against it. All these options seemed to be leading nowhere, Martin concluded. He had signed up that day in Bamenda to become somebody in this new company and somebody he was determined to become. But how? And when? He stood there and reflected some more

"What have you decided?" He heard the Black supervisor's voice loud and clear. This time the man was wearing a blue shirt with all five buttons on. Only two of those were not blue. Those two in a fine shade of green, blended with the blues in an odd manner.

"Please, sir, can I go back to the field and try again?"

The man nodded but sighed and closed his ledger. "I am giving you another chance, *you dis strong head boy*. But remember that our Ogas will not tolerate lazy men," he sighed. "Why are you so stubborn, na?"

As Martin made for the door the supervisor cleared his throat and spoke again.

"Martin, my boy, you should know that so far the company has employed ten book people. So be careful out there."

"Thank you, sir," Martin replied but felt a little ill at ease with this news. Ten literate men so soon? He pushed the door further to let himself out of the office wondering how badly this would affect his chances of becoming a Big man.

"Talk to your friend, John and see how he does it. That is one fine boy, a potential Big man the company is preparing."

Martin paused in his tracks. Weh! And what was he then? A mess! No, a Fear, Fear man. "Okay, sir. I will talk to him."

"Wait a second. Come back in for a minute, young fellow." The Big man invited him back. "Now how is Isaac faring in the hospital?

Martin hesitated.

"Uuh?"

Martin cleared his throat. "He says too many oversabi book people are there."

"I see!" He rubbed his forehead. "Yes, he did have a problem with those trained nurses who think they know it all?" The Big man nodded in agreement. Martin did not reply. The Big man shook his head while the corner of his mouth twitched.

"Now I remember it all. Yes, indeed!" He sat upright suddenly and stared right through Martin. "You know he is now in the research department working with those European scientists?"

"Yes, sir."

The man shook his head in disapproval. "I feel sorry for him but let him keep trying. One day, who knows?" He shook his head again. Martin waited.

"I am telling you, young fellow, field is the place to be. That is where I started; look at me now!" He grinned. He was about to say something when he caught sight of his European boss through a small hole at the back of his office beckoning to him. He jumped up at once and adjusted his tie. "Like I say, Martin, don't waste my time again." Martin had noticed the hole in the wall but had not fully understood its function. Until now he had only believed it was meant for mail. He left the room without looking back.

The second time around as a headman was not easy. Although he had carefully switched fields with a new recruit, word had already spread around that he was a terrible headman so the workers at his new post were waiting for him the first day at work.

"You there, this is where you end for today."

'*My name no bi 'you dere'*,'' the person replied.

"Okay, what is your name then?"

"*Ah no get name.*"

The workers thought this was a clever remark as they laughed.

"So you don't have a name then, eh?" Martin tried the next worker and the next but no one was willing to cooperate. He watched them disperse into the fields to perform their tasks just as they used to do under the previous headman. At the end of the day they walked over to the truck and boarded it without a word to Martin. He could not understand their behaviour. He stood by the roadside and watched them board in pairs, each helping the other onto the belly of the old rickety truck that continued to serve them well. He had to give it to them though; they had done the day's task with extreme care. Not one palm tree was left unpruned or ripe bunch of palm fruits left unharvested and hauled to the designated post. Martin got in and sat by the driver who looked away not eager to talk or to listen to Martin's stories. But Martin talked about the field experience anyway. The driver kept nodding and chewing on something. When he could handle the complaints no more, he advised Martin to take it up with the white boss. Martin thanked him. He felt good for the remainder of the ride back home. The driver must be on his side he assured himself and made a note to act on the man's advice as soon as he had the opportunity.

Later that night when he thought it over he developed cold feet. Why complain when the workers worked so hard anyway? Who would believe him? Martin dismissed the thought and slept well that night and subsequent nights thereafter. Another month came and passed and another and another, and soon he was getting the hang of things with this new team of harvesters but he was still tired of them pretending that he did not exist. In the fields he was the Big man, and they needed to understand that in that capacity he reserved the right to give them orders. Consequently, they needed to recognize that regardless of how good a worker each one of them was he could still sack them. They would not ignore him and get away with it. NO! So one day he made another attempt to exercise his authority as the headman but it got him nowhere. Frustrated with this constant display of insubordination, he threatened to report them. This did not work either. Instead, it intensified their contempt for his leadership. They ignored him and carried on with their daily tasks. He threatened them some more promising to write down names of those who disobeyed him in his ledger; still they did not warm up to him. Rather, they worked twice as hard so he would leave them alone. Martin was impressed with their work ethic but that was not what he wanted from them. He wanted more than that so he threatened them one last time. They had also had it with his attitude by now and so they decided it was time to act. They tied him up, threw him on the ground in broad daylight.

"*No bring dat your thing here-eh, Fear, Fear Head man,*" one harvester barked.

Emboldened by this the others cheered. They left Martin there on the ground and returned into the fields to finish their assigned task for the day. Martin wondered what they meant by 'don't bring that your attitude here!' What had they heard about him? Who had told them? As the Big man that he was he finally reported them to a Bigger man and a couple of them were fired. A week after the incident, a delegation of harvesters from his field paid him a visit at his home. At first, he was afraid that they had come to do him more harm. But the leader assured him otherwise. So Martin let them sit on his veranda and discuss whatever it was they needed to discuss. They asked him to go beg the white boss to reinstate the sacked workers.

"Mr. Martin, we beg you, sah!"

Martin could not believe it. He watched their contrite faces closely to see if there were any signs of sincerity. At first, he could not tell. But when one of them knelt in front of him, he was convinced and promised to do his best. And they left happily. But Martin could not deliver on his promise. His white boss told him he should use better judgment next time because anyone who got fired, remained fired. It was company policy and nothing could change that. Martin knelt in front of the man and pleaded on the harvesters' behalf in vain. Finally, he got up from the rough concrete floor and thanked his boss for his wisdom before leaving

When he related this to John that evening, John told him bluntly that it was time perhaps for him to admit that headman was not his calling. Martin felt a tremendous sense of relief and a few months later he was back in the Black supervisor's office where he got assigned to the hospital. He liked the new title they gave him: Dresser. But what he enjoyed the most about his new job was the fact that he had three sets of uniforms for work — all brand new. And his shirts were a good imitation of the Black supervisor's. Martin had finally made it or so he thought.

Chapter Four

H ey, you there, patients are waiting."

Martin stopped and turned around to face the speaker. "You mean me, sir?"

"Yes; who do you think I mean?"

"Are you not the new Dresser from the field?"

"Yes, sir."

"So patients are waiting for you. Go to the Out Patient unit, you lazy boy." With that the man walked away. Martin's immediate impulse was to insult this person, but he dared not. He had noticed the black name tag on the man's overalls – on the left breast pocket and guessed he was indeed a real nurse, not the type that learned on the job like him. So the most he could do was put his hand on his hip and curse under his breath. Then he left to perform his first medical task. There was a queue waiting there for him. Quickly, Martin put on his disposable latex gloves and waited for further instructions from another professional who stood there. From her red name tag he could tell she was a Sick Attendant. It brought a smile onto his lips. Lovely title, he mumbled. He watched her attend to patients with less complicated symptoms and illnesses, rashes here, malaria there, injection there. He loved what he saw. The Sick Attendant showed him different kinds of medications and ointment used for wounds and where to get instruments sterilized. Then she advised him to put a pad over his nose and mouth at all times.

"So what do I do next?" Martin dared to ask. The woman stopped what she was doing and stared at him momentarily.

"Just watch and learn," she suggested raising her eyes to the closest door.

"Next!"

A ten-year-old boy limped in."

"Put your foot on the stool," the Sick Attendant ordered.

"Now you sit still, you dirty boy." She examined the sore on his right ankle. It was already infected and had a foul odour.

"Why don't you people even wash before coming to consult na, eh?"

The child remained silent.

"Martin, give me the cotton balls. Wait, dip it in the spirit."

He did. "Now, give me the scissors and gauze and plaster."

Martin was confused. He fumbled around looking for the items.

"Over there," she directed him.

Martin handed them over to her.

When she touched the boy's wound with the cotton ball he screamed and tried to jump out of there. She slapped him across the face.

"You stop that at once. Don't you see that there is a lot of puss on your cut?"

The child nodded while whimpering. She added something on the gauze and wrapped some bandages around the boy's ankle.

"Now, you go and wait there for tetanus injection-eh?"

The boy nodded tears welling in his eyes.

"It will be better now, eh?"

The boy smiled.

The Sick Attendant turned around in search of something or someone. "Martin? Okay, now prepare the injection."

The boy started crying again.

"You stop it. If you were afraid of injection, then why did you have that smelly cut? Injection!"

Martin was mortified.

"Next."

As the next patient walked in the Sick Attendant read his hospital card closely.

"Hmm! Oga, big, big you too still get cut?" she was embarrassed that a grown man could have a wound like a child's. Martin was embarrassed for the man too. He could not understand how that could happen to an adult. Well, perhaps if the man had had some exposure to primary education this would not have happened. He empathized with him in his heart nonetheless, and paid attention to what the Sick Attendant was doing right there.

"My sister, leave me so-oh. No bi boil."

"Okay, show me the boil."

The patient took off his shirt and raised his arm. She touched it.

"Martin, you see how red it is?"

"Yes, Miss Agnes, I think it is done."

"You are correct. It is ready. Now ah go cut it with operation blade... Look in that drawer; give me a new one."

Martin did, getting ready to see her incise the boil to get rid of the puss.

"Give me injection let me kill this place so this man will not feel pain."

Martin brought a big one.

"Not that one, you fool." She got it herself, and did the incision in addition to everything else that was written on the medical card by the outpatient nurse. From the card the man did not need any tetanus injection. She returned his card to him and asked him to leave. The Sick Attendant attended to five more patients and stopped abruptly.

"Martin, now let me do my real work. *Na me di give the injection around here. You* Understand? I am the one who chooks people the injection!" She said it twice to make the point that she was his superior.

Martin was confused. "But I thought . . ."

"You thought what? That I would be treating wounds while you with no experience chook injections?"

"Not so, Madam."

"Go ahead, start treating people their wounds."

She stepped aside for him to proceed and headed into an adjoining room meant for those in need of injection. There she administered shots after shots. She could hear Martin's voice as it trembled whenever he said "Next!"

That day, Martin treated wound after wound. Fat ones, tiny ones, smelly wounds, infected wounds, bruises, boils, and so on. By mid day he was already exhausted from shouting at his patients and making them sit still for him to clean their smelly cuts. When he returned home for break he was sent to the male ward to assist the nurse in charge. This time he took temperatures and gave out several tablets of codeine, aspirin, camoquine, phenegan, alcopah until he threw up in the gutter. He had never touched that many medicines before. But the worst part of it all was taking bed pans for patients to use. At home that evening he could not eat. He had lost his appetite just spending the day at the hospital. But still it was too early for him to make up his mind whether to keep this new job or seek another one.

As his days as a Dresser turned into weeks and eventually into months, Martin began to get used to the hospital environment and realized that he could get the ward servant to do all the chores he did not like, like emptying the bed pans daily. His biggest triumph came when James had an accident in the fields and had to be hospitalized. That same James who had given him a hell of a time out there in the fields! It did not take Martin long to figure out how to get even. One evening before he left the ward, he walked over to James' bedside and read his chart out loud. It was all gibberish to James' ears.

"Hmm!" Martin looked concerned slapping his forehead repeatedly.

"James, doctor say they go cut your foot the day after tomorrow before puss spoilam." He lied as he attempted to frighten the man whose deeds in the fields while he was a headman remained ingrained in his memory.

"What?" James rose from the bed supporting his weight on his elbows.

"You heard me." Martin nodded staring past the wounded man. James looked dismayed at the thought of them amputating his leg and instinctively hung on tight to Martin's overall.

"My leg, Mr. Martin?"

"Uhuh."

"My Mami-eh! Mr. Martin, do something, ah beg." James screamed.

"Too bad! *Na so dis book say doctor tok*," Martin confirmed waving the chart in James' face and relishing the effect his lie was having on this man who was the most arrogant field hand he had encountered during his tenure as headman.

"Mr. Martin?" He pleaded.

Martin ignored him and pretended to read a section aloud: "Cut the leg before it rots!" His eyes now dead serious left the page and landed on the wounded leg. "This is what the book says."

"Weh!" James exclaimed resignedly.

Martin cupped his chin and waited before closing and placing the chart under his armpit.

"Mr. Martin, weh!"

"I understand, James." He replied edging closer to James who was now sitting upright with both hands clasped over his head.

" 'Cut my foot?' Ah beg you, Mr. Martin, do something?" James pleaded with Martin one last time. "Ah never even marry sef?" James rambled on and on about the doctor cutting off his leg when he was still single. They should at least wait for him to marry before they cut it. Martin listened patiently. When James was done begging, Martin stood up and like the Big man once more he patted him on the back and ordered him to conserve his energy. James lay still and waited. Martin was pleased with the power he now wielded over this stubborn man. He brought out the chart again and skimmed through it before returning. James' eyes followed Martin's movement helplessly.

"Okay, I will think about it. *For morning ah go tell doctor.*" He turned around to leave. "James, so you do understand grammar after all, eh?"

James was at a loss for words. He gazed at the Big man in stupefaction not sure about what Martin was referring to. Martin enjoyed the stupid look on James' face as he recalled how this same man had bullied him out there in the fields. However, it was only when he was in the hall that he let out a chuckle. He could not believe that James could be that gullible. There was nothing wrong with the leg; he wished he could tell the poor man the truth before he died from the thought of his leg being amputated. What a fool. Martin felt sad when he remembered how James had also made him look like a fool in the fields. He sighed, "poor man, to think that we shall cut his leg. What a shame!" He laughed and closed up for the day before walking gently home to join his family. He felt vindicated at last.

The next day, Martin accompanied the nurse-in-charge to James' bedside and explained his condition in rapid Standard English. The nurse nodded throughout and waited until Martin finished before examining James' leg. He turned it around a couple of times looking at the section that was red and getting swollen with puss and wrote furiously on James' medical chart. When the doctor came and read the chart he also scribbled something; each time this happened James' eyes followed Martin's every movement pleading for mercy.

"Martin."

"Sir."

"Go get the nurse."

The doctor handed over the chart and pulled the nurse aside to discuss the case some more. Martin saw both of them nodding and looking at him. When they finished conferring on the case the doctor left and the nurse walked over and handed over Martin a prescription. Martin dashed to the dispensary and returned with a handful of syringes and other medication.

"Now James, this should help you, eh?" The nurse-in-charge said as he administered the first injection. "Good; now this man here will take care of you, eh?"

"Yes, sah."

"Good." The nurse moved on to another patient leaving Martin to tidy up after him. Martin was happy.

"See, we just saved your leg."

"Thank you, Mr. Martin.

When James was discharged ten days later with his leg intact, he thanked Martin graciously and even suggested that he should come back to the fields. Martin was touched but said no. The hospital job suited him just fine. He did not have to spend hours sitting on rocks and waiting for the harvesters to finish their day's task. He liked sitting on chairs better and looking neat all day long and some days he even went to the hospital kitchen to eat a nicely cooked meal.

Life could not be sweeter, so Martin thought as a year came and passed with him getting the hang of his new position. It was now time for him to change houses so he would have hospital workers for neighbours. Martin packed and left without saying good bye to his former neighbours. He liked his new electrified two-room house and could not wait to make it look beautiful inside. Now he was beginning to feel important as he watched the company truck transporting his stuff across residential quarters with him sitting next to the driver and giving him instructions. He did not mind at that moment that he had left his friends behind. John did not care or if he did, he never showed this emotion. Isaac, Zacharias and Puis, on the other hand, were mad. And two weeks later, Puis returned to the Black supervisor's office to seek transfer to the hospital. His wish was granted much to Martin's dismay. But Martin taught him how to be a good Dresser the hard way making him do the tasks he had so graciously in the past relegated to ward servants. In spite of this Puis refused to quit this time or to change jobs. Within one month he had requested a change of house. His request was granted and he became Martin's neighbour once more. And so life went on . . .

Chapter Five

S ome months later, Martin sat down on his veranda playing draught with Zacharias, Puis and John. The twenty-four by twenty-four inch board sat carefully on their laps with the game pieces all in place Martin and his partner, Puis were losing again—as always! They had chosen the black chips as opposed to the white ones that their friends had always insisted on selecting. As he hung fervently onto his most prized game piece in a desperate attempt to save the game,

Zacharias coughed and burst into laughter. That same moment the factory clock chimed the time. He scratched his head and concentrated harder; but before he knew it, his game piece had taken the bait Zacharias and John had so carefully placed at one corner of the board for them.

"You die again!" Zacharias jeered rising up and checking his watch. His friends did the same. They realized that it was really getting late.

"Next time, na?"

"Yes, Zacharias, but it will be our turn to beat you people. Just wait and see."

They all laughed. "That is what you say every time, Martin. Well, let's just wait and see."

On this note Zacharias hopped onto his bicycle and began pedalling off alongside his pedestrian friend, John.

The next game was the same. Martin and Puis kept losing and losing but they never gave up. Rather, the more they lost, the more determined they became in their quest to defeat their two friends. Not a chance, Zacharias reminded them each time. And then one day, Martin picked up the board and really looked at the little white and black squares closely. He squinted and examined the board and that was when he realized that he could actually see Lobe estate on that board. It was a marvellous discovery to him. With his index finger he began tracing what he imagined were the different camps on the estate one at a time as he separated these fictional residential quarters according to professional ranks. Then, he looked at the squares again closely. He carved out a section there where he hoped to reside in the nearest future and muttered, "European quarters." he whispered.

His friends looked up.

"What?" Puis stood up in utter shock. But Martin simply sighed. He had never even been to that part of the estate. And he knew very well that neither had Puis nor the others. But from what the cooks, yardmen, washer men, and stewards had relayed to him, the place was heaven on earth! It would not be a bad place for him to aspire to, he decided. Martin looked around him. He liked his "temporary" residence. At least, everyone there could understand some form of Standard English unlike those in the camps he did not like to think about. He also liked his small house, which he had carefully furnished with good wooden chairs with spring bottoms and matching cushions. He even had a 'me and my girl chair' right there in his little abode. His kitchen was quite nice, better than what he had been used to before coming over in a truck like a cow, however, instead of firewood he had wisely bought himself a brand new kerosene stove that served him well. It was on this small stove that he fried ripe plantains and eggs for his breakfast each morning before going to work. Above all, he had bought himself a mighty four poster steel bed — Made in Nigeria. He concluded that he liked his life, at least at that moment. After all, he was still young and the Europeans would leave... soon.

His job, he was beginning to understand better and was now using medical terminology just like the professionally trained staff. So promotion was not that far off, he could see. Some days, he would go to the hospital primarily to order the ward servants who were only too eager to do as he pleased. He would lean against one of the hospital's metal poles along the corridor and with both hands in his white overall pockets, he would sniff the air for foul odour and shout: "Carolina?"

And the ward maid would rush in his direction right away.

"Wash, wash, wash!" he would order leaving the disoriented staff more confused as he headed to the male ward.

One day he heard that more hospital staff would be joining them in their residential quarters since there were vacant houses standing by. Immediately, Martin asked to be moved closer to the road. His request was granted and the very next weekend he packed into his new house. He counted the houses in the different rows for the first time and realized that there were twenty-one houses in total. Better to be in front than at the back, he assured himself as he settled into his new home waiting for life to hand out all the promises he had seen on the face of the recruit officer the day he had signed up to go down South.

"Pooooooh!" The factory would chime the six a.m. time to alert its workers of the beginning of the work day. Martin got up quickly and brushed his teeth on the veranda for all to see.

"Good morning-oh, Bessem," he greeted his unmarried neighbour holding his tooth brush firmly in his right hand and brushing vigorously.

"Good morning-oh, Martin. *You get tooth paste weh ah fit borrow?*"

He frowned not understanding how he could gently refuse her his tooth paste.

"*Na small one ah get,*" he responded letting her know that his tube did not have enough tooth paste for him to share. He enjoyed watching her go out and cut some hibiscus stems to use as a chewing stick.

41

"Good morning-oh, Oga," he greeted.

The Oga would nod in acknowledgement. *"You sleep well?"*

"Yes, Sir."

"Good."

At that point, he would then take a quick bath and go to work. Everyone knew his morning routine. Later in the day, he would wander into the hospital kitchen where he was certain to get something to eat. He was never disappointed. He worked around the clock paying close attention to the chimes from the factory that reminded workers of the time of the day. It made it easier for most, although Martin made sure he looked at his watch hour after hour to compare the accuracy of the official time and the one he had set on his watch.

The years passed by so fast and soon Martin started noticing pregnant women here and there. A colleague would go on leave and reappear a month or two later with a bride and a couple of months later the colleague would be a father sometimes of twins. Martin wondered what it all meant watching the excitement all over the hospital with the white doctor giving the couple lots of sweet smelling stuff to use on the child. The doctor had never noticed him even though he made sure he stood in his way every morning in the out-patient ward. The man would simply pass by him rushing toward a patient. When Martin mentioned this to his friends they all laughed and said it was the same thing at their sectors as well. Zacharias patted him on the back as he calculated his next move on the draught board.

"Massa, your own better" He concentrated on the board. Your situation is much better," he repeated in Standard English. "You see the man's face. What of me? All I hear once a week is his voice sounding through a hole as he ordered our Big Black supervisor."

John coughed. All eyes turned to him. "My own...," he hesitated. "You all know him na? That short man with big round stomach like that." They burst out laughing. "He

42

comes in his red Volkswagen and parks by the road and shouts 'Young lad, the book?'" He mimicked the man. "Then I take the ledger to him for verification. He looks at it and shakes his head. 'Make them work harder! No work, no pay!'" John mimicked the white field manager again and his friends laughed harder. "Then drives off."

Martin looked up at John. "He actually talks to you then?"

"Of course, na." John beamed with pride. Puis who had been quiet throughout the conversation cleared his throat. "John, that is nothing. Talk to our friend, Isaac. I think I'll go and join him at the research office too. *Ah tire this hospital work.* I am truly tired of it." He spat in disgust. "You know, Isaac says he works with his own white man in the same room and sometimes when it gets too late they roast mbanga and eat. White man eating palm nut? *Is what you are saying true so?*"

Martin nodded. "He is a scientist, what do you expect? I can swear that even though he is working every day in his lab with Isaac, he does not even see him. He does not even think about him."

Puis shook his head to the contrary. "No, no, no, you don't understand. They drive everywhere together. One day when you see a blue Volkswagen driving by just look. You'll see Isaac carrying some seedlings in the backseat!" He was so excited sharing this information as an insider.

"Oh, true, I have seen them many times then," John added. "I always thought that he had but seedlings in there. How can anyone breathe with those plants everywhere na?"

Puis jumped in again. "No, no, Isaac likes it. He says if he wanted to he could sit in front."

"I don't think so. You too! How can you believe that kind of a story na?"

"No, Martin. This man really likes Isaac-oh! He has already given him two tergal trousers and some white singlets."

"*Na true tok so?*" He turned toward his friend for more assurance that the information was accurate.

"Of course. I think ah go transfer for research soon."

Zacharias laughed. "Puis, if you keep changing, you will never give them time to even know you. So how do you expect them to like you?"

"*Ah go still try for transfer!*" Puis said this as he made a bad move on the board as well. And the game was over once again with Martin and Puis losing to their pragmatic friends.

As more hospital employees became couples or parents the peace that once reigned in the camp was disturbed. Instead of rising up each morning only to the chimes from the factory, Martin now got up to the sounds of babies crying or husbands beating their wives for one reason or the other. Before he knew it his neighbours were no longer stopping to chat as before and at work his colleagues ignored him more now. They were barely tolerating one another. The hospital meetings that were usually a formal event took a different dimension with the staff meeting now only for a short interval and less frequent. The doctor noticed this and added something new, for he said they needed to socialize with one another whether they liked it or not. Only he reserved the right to attend their social activities whenever possible. And so they added a mandatory annual picnic on their calendar, and always in the woods behind the doctor's house. Martin looked forward to these picnics, which gave him an opportunity to finally see where the Europeans lived. He liked what he saw. Then one day the doctor said they should change venues since the event brought too much noise in the area.

Thereafter, the picnics were held along the creeks with ferry boats transporting employees across the river and into the deep woods and eventually back to civilization. It was on one such event that Martin finally got the opportunity to shake the doctor's hands. When he mentioned this to his friends, they commended him for doing the impossible and Puis who had transferred over somewhere else was permanently stuck with the mean Black supervisor he had for a boss now – not the white manager he had fantasized for months and even years of working with in the same room. Worse yet, the Black office supervisor had scolded him for being too fickle and had bluntly told him that if he was not careful he would have nothing since there was a rumour that more educated people were being hired. "Real book people this time from college!" This frightened the five friends more than the ten literate people who had come after them.

Christmas that year for Martin and his colleagues was something special. The doctor threw a party for them in the hospital lounge and asked his wife to bring out the presents for him –now dressed as Father Christmas to distribute to all the children in there. Looking around there were less than ten children in the room, yet there were so many presents in the carton the doctor's house boy had brought into the room. Martin wondered what they would do with all the remaining gifts. He watched Father Christmas present gift number one to a little girl; she curtseyed as Martin believed her father must have coached her at home. Gift number two, three etc. he stopped counting and focused on the box watching a children's story book disappear, a toy car, a doll, a train set, a toy gun – wait a minute. Martin wanted that plastic gun for himself. He approached the house boy and whispered something into his ears. The house boy hid one of the toy guns for him for which he later collected some money from Martin. And so the Christmas celebration continued with the slaughter of a goat and roast pig served to all who were remotely affiliated with the hospital. The doctor proposed a toast to his staff and presented the medical superintendent with a new subscription to the *Nursing Mirror* journal.

Then dancing began and the doctor and his wife opened the floor followed by the medical superintendent and his wife then the five trained nurses and their partners. Martin watched in awe. He liked this and wondered why the doctor did not throw Christmas parties often. Another waltz tune was played with the same people on the floor while Martin and the others simply watched. When this was over the rest of the staff was invited to join in. But then only the few who could actually waltz could participate. Martin fidgeted on his seat. Around him those who mattered were waltzing, tangoing, rumbaing to the white man's music. He could see the doctor and his wife now sitting and watching the employees dancing. The doctor took a sip of his brandy and threw some biscuits into his mouth and laughed at something his wife said. The children had since disappeared, Martin could not even remember when. Things were happening too fast for him. Then the music stopped and everyone took their seats and waited. The doctor and his wife got up and waved everyone goodnight wishing them a "Merry Christmas."

Martin enjoyed every minute of it. One thing still bothered him though. He waited until the host of the party had left before summoning the courage to walk up to the person next in line.

"Sir," he began.

The medical superintendent looked at him.

"Oh, my boy, Martin, what is the matter?"

"Nothing sir," he hesitated.

"Sit down then young chap."

"Thank you sir."

"Okay, what seems to be the problem?" He sipped his brandy and licked his lips.

"That white man dance, sir; can you teach me."

The medical superintendent laughed.

"Is that all?" He laughed again.

46

"You know something, Martin, I did not get to be the assistant doctor for nothing-eh?" he sounded a little tipsy. "Of course, I will teach you a thing or two how to dance like a European. Eh?"

"Yes, sir." Martin was grateful. He did not want to be left out the next time the doctor decided to throw them a party of that magnitude again. He wanted to be part of the privileged crowd. So he would take the lessons regardless of the cost. He later recounted the experience to his friends who felt embarrassed for him.

"You say, only the assistant doctor and the professionals knew the steps?"

"Yes, Puis; and throughout I had a big head sitting there."

Puis nodded in sympathy. "I understand how you feel. Isn't that why you see me trying to work but with a European? I want to be like them. *Their dance fine; their house fine, their chop...* Everything about them is fine!"

They all looked at him funny.

"Okay, not their chop. Who even knows how their food tastes?"

Martin shrugged that off. He was not interested in their food. What fascinated him the most was their music and the steps that went with it.

And so a month later with the rest of the hospital staff, he started taking lessons. This new skill put them one step ahead again above their peers in the different divisions, for the following new year they out-performed everyone else at an annual New Year's Employee gala. This festivity became an estate tradition with each department head marking it on his calendar one year in advance to show the rest of the company employees how civilized they had become.

Chapter Six

One day John went to work as usual but was severely beaten up to the point whereby he was admitted to the hospital. He refused to tell anyone what had happened and refused to seek transfer elsewhere. He would not discuss it at all. Everybody knew he was the only headman who controlled more than five fields. In return he was rewarded with a Raleigh bicycle to facilitate his mobility from field to field. But what they did not know was that the fat, round belly white man who was the field manager had promised an increase in wages on condition that he put an extra eye on the workers to see who stole fruits. John accepted and had already reported three harvesters who had been warned to stay off "company property or else!" Two more violations and these employees would be sacked just like that! All because they stole a sack of palm fruits for their wives to prepare '*mbanga soup*' for dinner. But John was not so fortunate the next time. He was seen sneaking into the field manager's office with a ledger under his armpit a couple of times. One time, someone actually saw him talking through a hole to someone on the other side. And that was how the harvesters knew who the traitor was. It was a relief to those who had begun believing that the manager indeed did possess some form of magical powers, or else how would he know such things. A day after this discovery they ganged up and gave John a thrashing of his life. No explanation. No reason, just fist blows after fist blows on different parts of his body.

After three weeks in the hospital John was ready to go out there again to face his workers. When he arrived all ready to start bossing people around again, he realized that his boss who had not even bothered to show up to see how he was faring at the hospital had replaced him with a headman from another field. Why? He wondered. Did the manager have so little faith in his ability to heal so fast? John saw him talking to the new headman and immediately walked over to greet them.

"Oh, young chap, you're back!" The field manager said with a grin and asked for the big ledger. John did his job as usual but he now realized who the real enemy was – not his workers. It was clearly his own boss who could not even exercise his powers over a bunch of hooligans who had used their fists on him. So one day when he was off duty, John hid behind a palm tree and passed out excreta on cocoyam leaves and waited. He had heard that the boss always strolled in that area most evenings. So he waited for him there. It was his turn to take revenge. He could never understand why this man had replaced him just like that after he had been so loyal. Was he not a diligent worker? Had he not spied for the man? So why would he do that? Why could he not have waited for him to recover, but instead had hastily replaced him as though he was not an important man? These thoughts raced in his mind. He rubbed his eyes and waited.

He waited evening after evening. Then his opportunity came one evening and like a man he aimed the bundle of excreta right on the boss's face as he was about to kiss a white woman whom no one knew whether he was married to or not. Where John hid, he heard the woman utter a cry and spoke rapidly in English. Moments later he saw them driving off in their red Volkswagen.

"John, you are indeed a man!" John congratulated himself and came out of hiding. No one was going to use him like that and get away with it! Not even his boss whom he had secretly believed liked him and may become a friend!

The following Friday when they met for another game of draught he proudly told his friends how he made his boss to taste his shit. And the one who was most shocked by this declaration was Martin. He liked his white boss so much that he would never think of a mean trick like that. At first, he thought John was simply bragging but when the white managers rallied all the headmen for questioning about an assault of a superior, Martin realized that John had indeed done something terrible to one of them. The estate manager interrogated each head man in his office asking each where he was on that fateful evening. He spent an entire week questioning the men repeatedly in vain. Finally, as John related later to his friends, the manager gave all of them verbal warnings and promised to hold someone accountable should it happen again.

"Is this true so, John?" Martin was impressed. "Can he really catch you?"

John shrugged and smiled. "Let him try, if he is the Big man he claims to be." He smirked. "Let him try!"

The others stared at him.

"That night, I dressed like a harvester." He grinned.

"You did what?"

"My friends, I dressed like my workers. You should have seen me. You would have been proud of this man here," he said beating his chest. "I looked like them every bit with my raggedy shirt and foul smelling, worn out khaki trousers."

The others were dumbfounded.

He watched the expressions on their faces.

"I was one of them that day; every bit like the most feared one, so that even the boss could not tell the difference." He scratched his head. "What am I even saying? He did not have enough time to see me even. I was that swift in dealing the shit to them!"

They were shocked at the way he mentioned the foul word. But Martin was impressed. He patted his friend on the back. "You cunning bastard! Clever, clever chap." He paused. "Young fellow."

"No! Big man's nightmare," John corrected. "Now they will know who they are dealing with." He was pleased.

A few weeks later as they were returning home from work, they saw a plane taking off from the airstrip with a frightened looking white lady as the sole passenger. Martin immediately suspected she must be the woman John had told them about. So his friend had really done it. John had succeeded to drive the boss' wife or whomever packing out of the estate. Martin developed a new respect for John and concluded that he was Big man material.

As things calmed down John and the other headmen noticed a change in Mr. Crown. He stopped the casual chat he had occasionally with them whenever he came to inspect the fields. "John, how are your men today?"

"Fine, sir."

"Good. They look well and strong."

"Yes, sir."

"Good. Mbanga plenty today." He would look at the palm fruits at the drop off posts.

"Yes, sir."

But now nothing more. No more questions on how the harvesters were behaving or how they all fared out there in the heat or in the rain. Always 'show me the ledger;' he would cross check the figures, walk along a few sections of the fields to verify a few things and back to where the headmen stood. At this point he would nod and return the ledger with a grin. That was it. His recreational habits changed as well He now took along two ferocious looking dogs each time he went for his routine stroll, which were no longer as frequent.

With John's life back to normal, he went home to the village one day and returned with a wife. Martin looked at the small primary school girl John had for a bride and shook his head. Was his friend crazy? Why would someone not quite twenty-five want to be a father so soon? The others did not really mind. They simply understood that John would be John regardless of what they said. As a matter of fact it made them wonder about their own lives more. And so one by one they took in wives but for Martin who was still bent on enjoying his youth! He asked them once:

"If it's woman you people want, why don't you just go to the neighbouring villages and get some fresh, plump things like I do all the time?"

But John shook his head to the contrary. "You don't understand. Those plump things of yours; do they know how to pound achu?"

Martin thought for a moment and shook his head. "I have never really thought about that." He shrugged it off. "*Anyway, woman, na woman.* I don't need a cook; I just need one fine girl by my side. That is how I see it. Is there any difference between one woman from another?"

Zacharias laughed. "Perhaps so. *Those your local girls, do they know something sef? Only chop money, chop money! Ah tire them.* You think I haven't had my share of them?" He turned to another friend for support. "Will he not go broke one of these days?"

"Zacharias, is it not you who lets them chop your money?"

"No, no! They steal it from your valise, your trousers, your everything! They just steal it. Another thing is that when they cook who knows what kind of potion they put in there? Martin, ah don tire bachelor life-oh!"

With this he made one last move blocking Martin and Puis once more.

"Have you seen how they flood the estate on pay day?" Puis asked.

"They all want Sipec fish stew and rice; new brassiere like say my money has no work. Stupid things; do they think my money does not have work? Don't they know I have other things to spend money on?"

Martin giggled. What his friends said was true but taking in a wife — another person to feed and look after — that was just plain crazy! He dismissed the idea and changed the subject.

"Anyone coming for dance practice?"

"Of course, Martin."

"You too, John?"

John gave him a dirty look. "There must be something wrong with your head. You think I do not want to learn that dance too? Your head no correct!" He responded gesturing with an index finger the absurdity of the question. Only a man who wasn't thinking rationally would ask him that kind of question. He twirled his finger in the air next to his head to indicate that there was something wrong with his friend's thinking faculty.

"Okay, I get your point. I do have a brain you know."

"Good to hear that, Martin. For a moment I almost forgot."

The factory chimed the hour. Instinctively, Zacharias checked his watch.

"Mr. Martin, good evening-oh," a ward maid passing by greeted.

"How na, Miss Prudentia?" He replied.

"Ah dey fine," she smiled and wriggled her hip as she walked toward her one-room house three houses away. Martin watched her buttocks undulate as she walked away.

"Big man's food!" he sighed.

"What?" Zacharias asked bringing back Martin to his veranda.

"Oh, nothing."

Another colleague walked by smiling broadly.

"Martin, you people are still playing?"

"Yes-oh, Etey. How was work today?"

Etey still chewing on his chewing stick paused. "Martin, you yourself know how night duty is na? I've just finished a two-to-nine shift and now they want me to do night duty, a terrible shift as you already know." He sighed and shook his head in disbelief. "I don't know why they make me work so much. When I left Nigeria for this country, it was to do my normal share of work, not to be the company slave! If I knew it would be like this, I would have remained in Calabar-oh!"

"Eh-eh, Etey! That is how it is na. We all are workers, even the Europeans na?"

"My son, you've not seen anything yet. I have been a nurse all my life; no promotion; no special treatment. One white doctor come another go. The same mark time job..." he paused. "But I'm glad that I went to training school." Without wasting any more time he adjusted his white overalls and continued on his way home chewing his stick and humming a familiar tune.

Puis made another bad move. Martin had had it.

"Why do you play this game like jambo, eh? We are not gamblers; you should know that by now. Always gambling with your life and now you want to gamble with mine too? I don't want that."

"Ah, you too, Martin. See, I placed the game piece over there to trap them. You truly think I am a fool?"

"Yes," Zacharias jumped in laughing with a grunt. "Ah chop, chop and chop! He claimed the pieces he had won by avoiding the bait the others had carefully set up for him.

"But you expected us to play straight and land in front of that piece over there, no bi so?"

He laughed again. "I took the other road." Zacharias was very proud of himself.

"See, Puis, we die again! I wanted us to play..." Martin did not finish the sentence as someone was waving at him. He waved back.

"Mr. Martin, my sister says if you are hungry you can come and eat with us."

"Okay, Comfort."

"Mr. Martin, my mama says make you come help her change our bulb."

"Okay, Trisha."

"Mr. Martin, my . . ."

"Na wetin be this?"

He barked at the little boy who was trying to tell him that his shirt was ready and the mother wanted him to come pick it up.

"Martin this, Martin that; don't you all see that I am playing a game? What is all this rubbish?"

"No, you've just lost," John reminded him.

"Okay, so I have lost; so?" He turned around. "Hey, little boy, go and tell your Mami that I'm coming. Massa, these women with no husbands are too much.

What is hard in finding a man to take care of you?" His friends gave him a funny look as they wondered if he was okay. "Ah tire them! Too needy, these husbandless women!"

Then marry your own and they will leave you alone," Zacharias advised.

"Okay, I'll think about it then." Martin watched his friends leave.

"Maria, Comfort, Trisha, small Joe?" Martin ran off to perform all the little chores that these children had been pestering him with.

Day after day as the camp expanded with more children and ward maids with no husbands, he found himself eating here, sleeping there, breaking firewood here, keeping company there and so on. It was just too much for Martin and one evening he borrowed Zacharias' bicycle and rode all the way to Lobe town, a neighbouring village and returned with a girl – his latest girl friend. He told her she could stay for as long as she liked and that they could live as husband and wife. She accepted. But what he did not anticipate was her getting pregnant soon after the arrangement. So when she started spitting and throwing up two months after she had moved in with him, Martin did not know what to make of it. He asked her what was wrong and she said nothing. It was the right answer and it alleviated Martin's anxiety level for that moment. So he went about his business working hard all day and sleeping with her all night with no strings attached. It was a wonderful life, Martin thought. But his ideal life vanished one day when a female colleague in the maternity ward elbowed him in the hall and started smiling.

"What was that for?"

She continued smiling. "As if you don't already know, cunning man."

Confused, Martin followed her to the prenatal clinic.

"Your woman is in the family way. Let me be the first to congratulate you." She extended a hand for an appropriate handshake. Martin refused to take it.

"My woman? Which woman?"

"Your woman, na? Take my hand before it gets tired of waiting for the handshake."

Martin shook her hand. This was news to him. "My woman? Is this true, so? How can that be? Which woman, sef?"

The colleague stared at him in disbelief.

"You do not know the woman you put in the family way?" She took a step closer to hear his response. Martin said nothing.

"You sleep with your wife every night and you ask me a silly question? 'Which woman? My woman?' Eh?" She began wagging her index finger at him. "You better get out of my face before I do something crazy. 'Which woman?' You should be ashamed of yourself."

The colleague pushed him out of the clinic.

"But she is not my wife. She is a free woman! That is the truth," Martin shouted across the room. All the other pregnant women turned in his direction.

"What? Is it a lie?"

"Next," the colleague called out ignoring Martin. He noticed a woman pushing her way to the front to wait for further instructions. Her puffy face shone with grease. Martin grimaced and began tiptoeing away. With each step he took he could not help but wonder if the fathers of the unborn children those women were now carrying were aware of the pregnancies.

"Weh, what have I done with my life like this —eh?" he clasped both hands over his head and walked further away to face his future.

His worst fears were confirmed that fine day. "Your wife is in the family way," was all Martin could remember as he groped his way back to his ward. And that was that. Magdalene dropped out of primary school and became a full time house wife as she waited for Martin's baby. She asked Martin to go and see her relatives but Martin refused reminding her that they were not really married. She could not understand what he meant.

"How so?" she asked one evening.

"It is just so. You are a free woman."

"Na so you think?"

He looked at her strangely and wondered how she could even think that he would marry her. He thought of sharing this thought with her but decided against it.

"I am not seeing your people; case closed." He dropped the subject. She was perplexed at first at this behaviour but decided to give her man more time before she could bring up the subject again. So instead of fretting about the situation as the whole estate expected her to, she buried herself into house work, running the house her own way and counting the days and eventually weeks. Martin did not volunteer any information. She tried one last time to get the truth out of him, but he would still not discuss it. Finally, she shrugged off her disappointment and hoped he would be a good father.

For Martin, it was some kind of ill luck he could never fathom. Why did God have to punish him like this, he wondered? First, He had given him a good thing; now a pregnant woman? What use was such a woman to him now? He moved out of his bedroom and slept on the sofa in the parlour. But every morning when he woke up Magdalene's face was right in front of his, with accusing eyes just staring at him daily. At times, they would be so intense that he could actually swear they were burning a hole through a part of his body he was not even aware of. How could the small girl he impregnated unleash so much resentment in him? He stopped eating her food and stayed far away from her. This did not work, for whenever he was home she came looking for him. He stopped talking to her altogether but to his dismay her belly grew bigger with his child. In the evenings when Martin returned from work he would find Magdalene sitting on the veranda sewing. As soon as he stepped into the parlour she would drop whatever she was doing and serve him his dinner but Martin would push it away, hurriedly change out of his uniform and leave the house. And so their lives as man and woman continued until the day she went into labour. Martin was not around when this happened.

When the head midwife sent for him, Martin did not know how to respond to the news. He stood and waited in her office.

She smiled. "I see, you are finally here."

"Yes, Madam."

"Okay, I will take you to see her."

"Eh?" Martin pretended he did not know what she was talking about.

She went on anyway. "Come, my son. Let me take you to see your child."

"Child?"

She nodded. "Be happy; you are a Papa now."

He attempted a smile.

She laughed. "No, not that kind of happiness; shake skin; do something; drink, eat, dance. Whatever it is, just do something to show this happiness" she encouraged him.

Martin smiled again.

"More happiness. You know she is a young girl and the fat girl almost destroyed her private."

Martin winced.

"Now, you feel the pain. See! That's right, she made the sacrifice for you, not so?"

Martin continued to wince. The head midwife could not understand this kind of attitude from a new father.

"Martin, I order you to do something to show happiness. I order you to buy her something or else I will report you to the white doctor.

Martin did not want that. "Madam, she is not my wife. Why does everyone think I am married?"

"Is she not your woman? Did she not just give birth to your bouncing baby girl?"

She waited for a response but none was forthcoming.

"You must celebrate the birth, you hear me?" She pulled her right ear. "Or the doctor."

"Madam, why do you bring our white Oga into this na? No need for that. I will treat her well."

"Good. Now my own drink for the celebration is a bottle of schnapps."

"A bottle of schnapps will be here tomorrow."

She smiled and dismissed him with a nod the way Big people do when they no longer needed the services or attention of the little people.

"Go see the baby and the young Mami."

Martin thanked her and left.

A week later when Magda was discharged from the hospital, her mother and two sisters moved in with them in the two-room house to help. They did not ask Martin's permission before inviting themselves into his house. All that mattered was that they daughter and sister needed their help and they were going to offer their services. True, Magda was not legally Martin's wife, but as he himself acknowledged, she was his woman and they were her relatives. Martin did not seem to mind this intrusion from his woman's relatives at first very much, for they spent their time cooking one delicious meal after another, washing his clothes, and looking after Magda and the baby. But then he witnessed them de-shelling snails in his beloved kitchen one evening. That was it. He told them to pack and leave his house, for he was a graffi man who did not condone snails in his pots. His woman's mother told him off calling him a foolish man. How could he live with their daughter and not want them to feed her with the very meal they had raised her on?

"Magda, this your Martin na foolish man." She addressed her daughter instead ignoring Martin completely.

Martin restrained himself for a couple of weeks watching his woman's relations stroll from his kitchen into his bedroom and back to the parlour ransacking his entire house. The little privacy he had with Magda was no longer there. They wore whatever footwear they found in the house. Martin got tired of this and exploded one evening hitting the table hard. "No more of this rubbish in my own house." The baby stared and started crying.

"This is my house, Magda; tell your people so."

The women were astonished at this behaviour.

"What is wrong with you, Martin?" Martin's woman's mother asked.

He ignored her and continued screaming beating his chest loud as well.

"Magda, talk to your foolish man. Something seems wrong with his head."

"Magda, you hear how your mother speaks about me?" Not waiting for a response he faced the woman. "Did you all come here because you thought I was a foolish man?

Eh? And you Magda, is that why you managed to get pregnant one, two, three times we were together?"

Magda's mother dropped what she was doing and stood up to face Martin. "You, Martin, you be foolish man. Magda, where are you?" The older woman turned looking for her daughter. Martin seized that moment to storm out of the house.

"Mami, see what you have done." Magda ran after Martin but he had already disappeared.

"Mami, you get for listen for Martin," Magda cautioned. "He is not a bad man."

"Listen for who? That foolish man who eats crickets?"

"He is not a foolish man and you know that."

"You are also a foolish daughter. Always have been and always will be." At that, Magda's mother ignored her foolish daughter as well.

It was a different life Martin was experiencing and as such the usual Friday games had been transferred over to Puis' house. They would meet there each week and play their game silently then Zacharias would tell a joke about Martin's house hinting that it was packed with female strangers just waiting to please him. "Really, Martin, how do all those women taste? The same?"

Martin did not find this funny.

"Zacharias, you are looking for trouble-oh!"

"Okay, I hear you. But, boh, the little sister must taste better na? Eh? Or you have not yet had the opportunity to try this fresh, plump thing that sleeps in your parlour?"

The others looked up.

"He has a point-oh, boh!" John concurred.

Martin ignored them. They continued to tease him week after week letting him know what they thought of him and how they felt about him. Too many innuendos got into Martin's head and one night he actually did it to Magdalene's younger sister right there in the parlour. When Magda caught them red-handed she beat her sister up and asked all three of her relatives to leave her house. The mother cried a bit, laughed a lot and then congratulated herself for having produced such attractive daughters who drove both sensible and foolish men crazy. She was one proud mama.

When they all left Magda's daughter was already crawling but Magda was still too sour from the experience of catching her sister and her man in bed. She moved around sulking daily and not bothering to prepare the kind of special dishes she used to fix for Martin before. He noticed and asked her why. She ignored him. Martin, tired of her attitude, rode three miles to her village every Saturday to visit with her relatives. What started initially as a way to get good meals and some attention from Magda's relatives eventually became a habit, and he enjoyed it and looked forward to the weekends. He had been going over there for a couple of months when one day they greeted him with the news that Joanna, the younger sister was carrying his baby. Martin rode right back as fast as possible into the arms of Magda and never returned to the village. But then months later Magda's mother came over to the hospital bringing Joanna to deliver Martin's second child. When they arrived, Martin's woman's mother announced that it was Mr. Martin who had impregnated her little daughter, so Joanna deserved all the benefits that befitted her as the expectant mother of an employee's unborn child. The head midwife said that was nonsense since Martin already had a woman. Joanna's mother acknowledged this and reminded the Big woman that regardless of whether another woman lived with Martin or not, her second daughter was expecting Martin's child.

"So?"

"Na his child."

The head midwife dropped what she was doing and sent for Martin and he came running to explain. When he arrived panting the head midwife cast one look at him and wrote something in her ledger.

"Is this your wife, now?"

Martin hesitated taking a look at Joanna now heavy with child.

"No," he said and turned around to leave.

"Mr. Martin, you tell them the truth. If she no be your wife, then the belly came from where?" Martin sighed. He was getting tired of this game.

"Madam, I do not have a wife!"

The head midwife noticed the strain in his voice as the veins popped up around his neck. She jotted something down again in the ledger. "But is this another one of your women?"

Martin remained silent. The head midwife got the message.

"You are such a foolish man, you this Martin. Don't you want a real wife?"

Martin scratched his head.

"Madam midwife," Joanna's mother began. The midwife turned in her direction.

"Joanna no want marriage. Just for her child."

The head midwife was uncertain.

"Madam, ah beg you, money no dey for clinic. We have no money at all, unless Martin . . ." she paused in the middle of the sentence, fixing her eyes on Martin. "You this Martin, I still say you be foolish man."

The midwife began writing furiously stopping to eye Martin with disgust. When she was done she looked at the two women who needed her help.

"Okay, Joanna. Just this time, you hear?"

"Yes, Madam."

"But we go cut the money out of Martin's salary." She faced Martin, running her eyes from his toes to his head.

"Martin, and you call yourself a man?" She spat out with contempt,

Martin mumbled.

"What did you say?"

"Nothing, Madam."

"I thought so. Take your bad luck and leave my maternity before I change my mind and do you harm."

He left the office quietly. When he was in the hall he scurried off, panting all the way to his ward and hid in the bathroom. He did not want to have anymore conversations about Joanna and her pregnancy. He waited there for awhile wondering why he was so unfortunate. There was no one there to help him figure this bit out for him, so he dropped the thought and came out of the bathroom to resume his duties as the dresser he was.

On that fateful day Martin returned home only to find a gathering of women on his veranda with his female colleague exclaiming and using profanity repeatedly. As he approached the veranda she paused for a moment to spit on the ground rolling her eyes in disgust.

"What now?"

"As if you don't already know."

He brushed her aside and entered his house. He could see pieces of luggage on the floor in his parlour.

"What is this, Magda?"

"Don't touch my bundles, you hear?"

He went into the bedroom and came out again unsure as to what to do.

"What is happening?"

Magda ignored him as she carefully saddled her daughter on her back and began dragging her belongings she had carefully arranged in old loincloths.

"If you are leaving, don't you think I should know?"

"You already know." She sighed and stepped out into the yard with the women on the veranda cheering her up.

"Go you, my sister."

"Thank you, Ma Trisha."

Martin followed her out in the yard. "Magda, really what

wrong have I done? Even if I had killed someone, is this how you treat someone who fathered your child? Eh?"

She dropped the bundles down.

"Martin, you so, leave me alone-oh!" She wagged her index finger at him.

"But what did I do now?"

She grabbed one of the hands he was waving in the air as he claimed ignorance of any crime and sank her sharp teeth deep into his flesh.

"Stop it," he yelled at her wrestling his hand out of her mouth.

She bit him again.

The baby began crying and Magda gave up and directed her attention to the baby who was fastened on her back. Moments later she was gone from Martin's home.

But Martin rode all the way to the village to assure her that she was the one he wanted and not the younger sister. Magdalene did not believe him and refused to return to his house. Her mother sided with her so he left without her and carried on as if nothing had happened. When he related this to his friends, they advised him to forget about her. He saw some wisdom in their advice and decided to lead his life accordingly without Magda. It was very predictable; he worked, visited with his friends and returned home late to rest. He liked it this way and was beginning to get used to it. But one evening when he returned home from work he found Joanna sitting on the veranda sulking.

"Now what? Have I not taken good care of you?"

She sighed. "Just open the door."

He did and she moved in with him.

"What are you doing?" Martin asked the following morning when he noticed her unpacking her clothes.

She ignored him and continued rearranging her dresses and other personal items in his bedroom.

"Joanna, I do not like this one bit!"

"Like what?"

"What you are trying to do."

She ignored him.

"You know say this is Magdalene's room, not so?"

"So?" She brushed him aside and made more room under the bed for a fertilizer bag she had brought along with her.

Martin had no choice than to live with Joanna. To prove his love for Magdalene he began spending weekends at her village with her not bothering to inform Joanna about his whereabouts. Joanna suspected nonetheless, and did the only think she could do. She hid his notes that he had been studying in preparation for an upcoming exam for promotion. He flunked the exam and quietly continued his job as the dresser. Only now a ward maid he had disliked with a passion had been promoted to his rank. This angered Martin so much that for the first week he refused to teach her the basics of the new job. Worse yet, she and Joanna became lunch buddies sitting on his veranda and gossiping over meals on a regular basis. So wherever he went he ran into her. There was no peace for him. Then one day he had a brilliant idea. Martin slept with her and just like that made her realize who was the master once more. Had he not seen her naked? Of what could she be arrogant about again? It was indeed a brilliant idea to contain the boastful young woman, and it worked like a charm. Peace was restored once more into Martin's professional life.

When Magda had a second child – a boy this time, Joanna disgusted, left Martin for good. Still Magda would not return to *that* house. Instead she demanded a steady allowance with which Martin complied, and although this made her extremely happy, she never had a change of heart about returning to Martin's house. It was absolutely unnecessary she told him. But she would remain his woman for as long as there was the need. Martin did not understand what that meant; neither did he press further for her to explain what she meant.

Chapter Seven

M artin, you have failed again. What's the matter with you?"

"Sir, I don't know-oh. But some people say it is Joanna that is witching me. You know, sir, Magda's sister."

The superintendent shook his head in disapproval. "See, these local girls are trouble. I always warn my staff to be careful how they follow those women. See! How can you fail a simple exam like this? Even ward servants know that when one steps on a nail you need to give him anti-tetanus, right away, eh? And how can she really bewitch you?"

"Sir, I thought I wrote it down correct."

"No, you didn't. Perhaps you should go back to the field." The medical superintendent looked disappointed. He stared at Martin intensely. Martin's eyes reddened.

"You see, we don't want day dreamers in this hospital. Out there in the fields, you can day dream and you will not kill someone, eh?"

"Please, sir, not the field again. I beg of you sir; I will even lick your feet if you let me write the exam again." He dropped onto his knees and pleaded. "Weh, sir! field sir, you know how it is over there; they throw shit on your face; they beat you there; rain falls on you there all the time. Help me, sir. I don't want to spend my life drinking garri every afternoon." At this point he was already hugging the man's boots.

"Alright! Another chance then. You know, if you fail this one the doctor will sack you just like that." He snapped his fingers. "What am I even saying; I will sack you just like that. Go, go, go!"

"Thank you, sir." Martin headed out of the office shutting the door behind him. Eight months later he wrote the exam again and passed with flying colours. When the results were released to the rest of the hospital staff Martin was made a Sick Attendant. He never touched smelling sores again. He felt proud of himself and completely forgot about the two women who almost ruined his life. Later when the company sent out painters to repaint the houses Martin asked that his should be painted red. When they enquired why? He said it should be a sign of danger to any woman who dared to chase after him. The painters understood. But this still did not deter Magda and Joanna from dropping in every pay day to demand money for one thing after another. And so it went with Magda knocking on the door and finding her way into the parlour to wait for a couple of hours until Martin gave her what she had come for. Then it would be Joanna's turn. Ironically, they took the money without a word about the children. Martin did not seem to care either. He simply gave the money and watched them leave his house the same way they had come in wriggling their buttocks vigorously. Not a word about the children he had now fathered with the two sisters.

He liked it this way and quietly reminded himself that it was easier to pay them monthly allowances for child support than to have either of them under his roof again, even though he had spent months praying for Magda's return.

Believing that he had truly taken control over his domestic space and professional life he enrolled in more dance classes. The more he learned how to waltz the more his interest in the dance lessons increased. In no time he became the best dancer in the hospital. Everyone was impressed, including the doctor who had nodded in approval during one of the social functions. But Martin had no steady partner. So whenever there was a dance event as was usually the case, he would waltz himself to the door of an unmarried colleague and curtseyed smiling all the way and saying in the most polite voice, "Please, can you be my partner this evening when we go quick, quick slowing?" And the woman would laugh and respond "You dis Martin-so; Na white man you want be? Why you no di marry na? Just get married and leave us alone." But she would oblige him and be his partner. He enjoyed his social life, for single professional women scrambled for him as their dance partner all the time. They enjoyed the passion he brought to the dance floor leading them through the foreign dance steps without a care. Martin was on top of his game as a dancer on the plantation. He knew it and suspected those who matter secretly acknowledged his superior skills in this domain even his close friends.

All was fine with Martin. He was so content with his life and accomplishments that he actually forgot about the two sisters who had almost derailed him. At twenty-seven he now looked dashing and polished, and had become every woman's fantasy on the estate. Then one day during a draught game at Puis' place, John and Zacharias announced their good news. It was real good news, the kind that Big men cherished above all things; important news that little people simply dreamt about all their lives. John had been promoted to the rank of an overseer and now had a Honda motorcycle; Zacharias was now on category six and had even overheard the white man whispering through the hole to the office supervisor to put an eye on "that young chap who is full of promise!" That day, drunk by their success they beat Martin and Puis not once but six times at their draught games. Puis who had failed his bar exam for the second time and had refused to go for the third and perhaps last time froze.

"Boh, Martin," Zacharias began. "Sometimes, I wonder why you people keep losing like this. Is it the colour... Here, here, take our white buttons and we'll take your charcoal black things. Eh?"

"Ah! Go there Zacharias; what kind of name is that even?" Martin feeling resentful brushed off his friend.

"Don't spoil my name-oh. I am not responsible for you people failing your exams all the time." Zacharias chided stretching his arm. "I think it's just plain dullness because even my little Tomas who is only two-years-old can beat you in draught."

All was calm for a while but they could each sense the tension that was slowly building up that afternoon as they played their game. John began packing the chips and hurling the board away from their laps. Puis went into the house, said something inaudible to his wife and returned with bloodshot eyes. They could smell schnapps on his breath.

"Now you all, get out of my house!"

They were shocked at this outburst.

"Ah say, get out of my house. After all, it is not you people who are feeding me. Go away. Some bush thing them sef."

"Ah, ah, boh, what did we do na?"

"Martin, you too get out. So I failed my bar exams, don't I have the right to fail too? Don't I have a two-room electrified house like you too? So what if you all are on categories five and six? I even eat better than you people. Get out!" He screamed at them.

"I am tired of you all bragging all the time. Even you too Martin who has bastard kids all over the place, you don't even have shame. You come and insult me in my house; get out!"

John mounted his new Honda 125 started it and let it roar for ten minutes or so disturbing the peace further. Before taking off he screamed at his friend, "Oh, life is so sweet. Ah tell you people, it is people like us who will take over from the Europeans!"

"Yes, go. Some dirty thing sef." Puis barked back at him.

Zacharias took his time to leave. "Puis, what is really your problem?"

"Just go, and take that your stupid game."

"Alright, but with your fashion like this I don't think we are going to let you join the staff club!" He cautioned and began to leave. Puis peeped through his door blind and saw them leaving. "Staff Club my foot. We all know that there's really one good club – European club – and we all know say we are fit only for the bed bug club, which they were kind enough to give us. Staff Club my foot!"

"Zacharias, what staff club?" Martin asked walking away from Puis' accusations.

"Our own club to stay away from people like you, Martin. Yes, I have said it."

"What?"

Zacharias hurried away. "Are you a staff, eh, Martin? Not to talk of your friend over there driving us from his house."

Puis now very angry came out with a machete to chase them further away his property. Martin and Zacharias dodged his first aim.

"Puis you must be out of your mind," Martin attempted to wrestle the machete out of his hand.

"Are you a staff? Martin, let the baggar cut us. You see why we need to stay away from people like you? Bush man who thinks that he needs to solve every problem with a cutlass!"

"I am not; but you will never be a white man no matter how hard you try. And you too, Martin, you can waltz all you want, you'll never be one. Stupid imitation white men!" The machete was on the veranda now but Puis was fuming with anger. "Take your imitation faces out of my yard, chaps. Baggar them sef, or is it burger? I don't even know what those people even say."

"We hear you, Puis; Martin, make we go."

Martin followed Zacharias all the way to his three-room house in Staff quarters pleading along the way that when it came time to selecting members Zacharias should not overlook him; after all, he knew how to waltz, tango, rumba, and even how to dance soukous. Zacharias nodded as he pleaded. "My friend I know all that na, but it will still be tough. Your hospital bosses are behind this. They clearly said 'Staff Only' you know."

"Boh, weh, try hard to get me in the club, ah beg you."

They parted that night with Zacharias still unable to make that promise. But Martin was convinced that his friend would do something on his behalf.

Martin had not fully recovered from the possibility of not being selected as a member of the pending staff club when panic hit the estate. A fleet of military trucks with thousands of gendarmes drove through the estate and camped out by the creeks waiting. Nobody knew what they were waiting for. Then the rumour began. Nigeria was on fire! Before the heads of the different sectors of the company could alert their workers, news of people being raped started spreading. First, it was rumoured that the Estate manager's cook had raped the yard man's daughter. The research manager's steward had cracked open the cook's skull; an arm had been broken here, a leg there. It did not take the white managers long to figure out what was happening. The Ibos, Amaseres, Ibibios, Hausas, Ijaws and others who cleverly neglected to specify their ethnicities to the white managers were having their own war right there. So they were given an ultimatum: either they lived in peace or they would all be shipped back to Nigeria to participate in the war. They made their peace and the Big bosses left them alone.

Day after day, there was panic as Ojukwu did something or Gowon did something. Some workers even believed that some of their bombs would find their way to Lobe, so Field one was completely abandoned. The harvesters threatened to feed John to the crocodiles in the neighbouring rivers, if he dared to make them go near that Field. He succumbed and left them alone. Their fears were somewhat confirmed when day in, day out the gendarmes and marines retrieved floating corpses or floating body parts from the creeks. The hospital became as busy as a beehive. Orphans were being hurled out of capsized boats and brought over to the hospital. Night and day they emerged, some with claims of having swum all the way across the creeks. Mothers, students and sometimes 'cowardly' men too would be picked up escaping from the war. And so the entire estate became a major refugee camp. Martin had no choice but to make room for four orphans. Everyone had an orphan but for the Europeans. It was demanded and expected of company employees to be kind to these people who were fleeing from the dreadful war. The ambulance never seemed to stop sounding its imitation siren.

At nights, Martin would hear Mr. Okon quarrelling with the young Ibo ward servant over something. And when they asked him in the morning he would grumble that the boy was a greedy Biafran and that was that.

"Etey, why you say something like that na?"

"Martin, you be small boy, what do you know? Those people cause trouble too much. I don't know why assistant doctor even give that baggar job sef! One day when Gowon defeats that Ojukwu that is when they will come to their senses."

Martin left it at that. Like the rest of the workers he did not know what to believe anymore. Some said it was Gowon who started the war; others said it was Ojukwu. That was none of his business anyway! He just wanted them to stop fighting so the orphans in his house would leave. He did not care and was not interested to know who the trouble maker was! He would get up every morning to buy "puff puff" for his four foster children. They would eat this fried, round sugar pastry hungrily and sit there looking at him for more. He did not understand why they could never get satisfied with the food he offered. At first, he would buy eight for them to have with their tea for breakfast; then he realized that they were never full. He increased the quantity and kept increasing it and finally one day when he ran out of change he said enough was enough. He barked at the oldest, a ten-year-old boy who had gulped down ten puff puff all by himself. The boy ran out screaming for help. Martin charged after him.

"Make wuna war finish let all these gluttons carry their langaa throat and leave my house. Was it me who caused the war? Your papa them ran out of money to feed you then they start fight war so other people will raise you people eh? Yes, I have said it; let this your people's war finish soon."

"Papa Martin, ah beg no vex. Na hungry. Biafrans na dier work.," One of the children pleaded kneeling on the floor with her hands clasped over her head as she blamed the Biafrans for the war.

"We be orphans, na God's work."

Martin stormed out of the parlour. "God's work my foot. You there, what's your name again?"

"Peter, sah"

"Now, you take this money and go buy garri and sugar. From today onwards no more puff puff and tea. Garri and sugar. Ah tire. Just one month I have already spent..." He tried to calculate the amount in his head but gave up. "I have spent more than I make."

The children pointed out the one whom they identified as the most gluttonous.

"Now get out of my sight."

Martin had never been so furious. He was too overwhelmed with the responsibility of taking care of these strangers. When would God reward him? When exactly, he wondered out loud. But his neighbour, Trisha's mother advised him to reward himself in the process. That he should never complain but to simply do what she did or else the government would take the children away from him. He laughed. That was exactly what he wanted. Someone should relieve him of this burden. He wanted his house back free of children as it was and not smelling of urine everywhere because the children were too afraid to get out at night for fear a bomb might drop on their heads. Lies! Those bastards take him for a fool. No more! He would like them out of his house, especially Chinedu. That boy could finish a basin of garri at one sitting and still not be full in the stomach. A boy who never complained of hunger but who never denied his stomach food even after eating a whole pot of jollof rice all by himself!

Trisha's mother pulled Martin inside her bedroom and gave him more advice. She told Martin that she had asked for six more orphans. Martin was astonished. How could she when she already had her three children and five orphans? How could she? He looked around the already crowded room and sighed. She must be insane to keep requesting for more. Not him! Then she revealed the truth to him.

"Martin," she began. "Orphans are not used to good food like regular people," she laughed. "Especially these ones from the war zone. They eat garri or pounded cassava with any soup. Okay, Ijaw people eat fish, so what; but ah tell you load their bellies with garri and okro soup and they will be fine. Just tell your four orphans to join my own to go look for wild cassava in the bushes."

Martin was appalled at this idea.

"Your head no correct. You want me to send people's children in the bush? Have you truly lost your senses?"

Trisha's mother laughed. "What are your options? Spend more money on puff puff and rice?"

"I will do no such thing." Martin was adamant about this.

"Then join forces with me. Just tell them to harvest the cassava with my orphans, eh?"

"I don't know-oh."

"What don't you know, you this weak man? Eh?" She was beginning to lose her temper.

"Okay, I am sorry I called you a weak man. But see my point too. These children from the war zone are strong-eh! They can work until you fear. So just show them how to find the food and they will do it. Eh?"

Martin nodded resignedly. What was the point? He was fast running out of money anyway.

"Good. These are some leaves we eat in Mamfe. Show them and they will recognize it, so that when they go to the bushes they can also search for these vegetables."

Martin looked at her oddly. He would never understand this coastal woman. She gave him more survival tips.

"Why do you do this, Bessem?" he asked Trisha's mother.

She laughed. "What kind of question is that? You do what you have to do to save money, don't you?"

He shrugged his shoulders.

"Okay. I have a plan, more plans for my orphans but I will keep it to myself. After all, I don't trust you 100%. But Martin, whatever the case don't let government know that the children are more than you. You know, they will reimburse us when this is over. You know that, don't you?"

Martin did not know. It was the best news he had heard since he started taking care of the orphans. He thanked her and returned home next door to get organized. He had to start keeping detailed accounts of everything that he had spent and would eventually spend. Taking Bessem's advice he made Chinedu the leader of the orphans and gave him instructions as to what they were supposed to do. From then on whether they ate basins of garri or cassava at one go, he did not care. They were worth every coin and sweat they had all put in making it happen.

He could not remember how long the children had been with him when one day he returned home and found a woman sitting on his veranda. She had a big satin headscarf on her head and a white lace blouse over her neatly tied George wrapper. She looked so prosperous Martin hoped it was one of the government officials coming to reimburse him. When she saw him walking toward the house she smiled. Martin smiled back. "What can I do for you, Madam?" He asked mounting the two steps that led onto the veranda.

"Na your salute that? Mr. Martin, you know I am a business woman from Kumba. Greet me well."

"Good day then, Madam."

"Greetings to you too, son." She cleared her throat and smiled. Martin waited for her to say something.

She smiled again. "Of course, you already know that I am from out of town. I just wanted to thank you for taking care of my Ngozi. You see, my sister and her husband were coming to join me when their canoe capsized. But God was so kind..." she paused to make the sign of the cross; "small Ngozi just floated on an empty kerosene tin. All these months I did not know she was even alive until yesterday." Tears welled up in her eyes.

"Come in then, Madam. Sit down for chair make your wrapper no spoil. I would be ashamed if your clothes got ruined by my old chair."

"Thank you, my child." She looked around the parlour with great admiration.

"Where's Ngozi?"

"Ngozi," Martin called.

The little girl came running into the house. When she stepped into the parlour, the older woman burst into tears rambling in Ibo and making more signs of the cross. But Ngozi had never seen this woman in her life. She started recoiling and heading out of the door.

"Ngozi, stop there." She stopped and waited for more instructions. The older woman stood up and embraced her fondly in a desperate attempt to assure the girl of her love for her but Ngozi froze. She waited for Martin to do something but he simply watched the family reunion. Next thing, Ngozi was in a 404 Peugeot heading for Kumba with the richly attired woman and her chauffeur. She kept waving at Martin until the car completely disappeared. Martin wondered if he had done the right thing in letting her go. He felt sad as he dropped on the sofa where the woman had sat. As he adjusted his buttocks to the contours left behind by Ngozi's aunt he felt something hard. He stood up and searched the cushions and underneath one he found an envelope addressed to the woman. Martin opened it slowly and out fell a picture. He picked it up and looked at it closely. It was a picture of Ngozi and a younger version of the woman who had just left his house. He heaved in a deep sigh of relief and searched for more pictures. There were two more of people he could not recognize. Martin could relax now and decided to concentrate on the other orphans. He concluded she was one less charge to be bothered with. But he missed her terribly still.

So weeks later he started mailing her bottles of aspirin and alcopah to keep her healthy. Ngozi's aunty wrote back to thank him and to let him know that he was welcome to visit anytime. Martin was pleased to read this in the letter. Two other orphans under his charge left the same way; and finally someone came for Chinedu. Martin heard tires screech not too far from his veranda. As he stood up to see what was happening out there, he saw a stout man emerge from a brand new truck. Martin sat down and waited and surely there was a knock on his front door. When Martin opened the door, the stout man in a well-tailored jumper stepped in. Without waiting to be offered a seat, he sat down waving a hand for his companion to wait outside with the others. Martin watched the man settle comfortably into the cushioned chair he had selected for himself, before asking who he was and what he wanted. The man announced that he was a relative and that he had spent several months waiting around the creeks for Chinedu whose parents had written to him that the child was on his way to the Cameroons. Martin was touched and asked Chinedu to get a cup of water for the guest. The man gazed at the coffee table where Martin had placed the cup of water for him to quench his thirst. He ignored the water and focused on his mission. He explained further why he was there. On hearing this Chinedu cleared his throat and dropped on his knees and began pleading that his Master should not hand him over to the stranger.

"Yes, Chinedu, you have to go. This man is your father's cousin. You must do as he says."

"No, Massa, ah no, know him. See his face. Na Moonchi man, no be Ibo!"

The man's face contorted hearing the boy challenge his claim of being an Ibo man.

"You are really a bad boy. Bad, bad pickin!" he repeated in pidgin .

"No doubt your papa dem send you make fish dem eat you in that infested river. You should be grateful that I, your father's cousin want to look after you in this stupid country. See this man standing here that you call 'Master,' na Cameroonian! Me so," he said drumming his chest proudly. "I am your own blood relative. Foolish, ungrateful boy!. It is your mother's bad blood that is making you so stupid. Oya, get up let's go." He stood up at once.

"No." The boy attempted to run away. The stranger grabbed him by the shoulder.

"Where do you think you are going?"

"Chinedu, do as he says."

"No, Massa! That man di lie. Na Moonchi or Ogoja, no be Ibo proper." He tried to wriggle himself out of the man's grip but could not. The man snapped his finger and the chauffeur and two hefty young men slightly older than Chinedu walked in and grabbed him. Martin was shocked.

"Who are these people that you are bringing into my house?"

The man ignored Martin.

"Take him away," he ordered.

They dragged Chinedu out of there like a captive and dumped him into the back of a pick-up truck that was waiting for them right out in front of Martin's house. Martin was confused. He followed them out of the house.

"Oga, but why do you take a boy who says he does not know you, na?"

The man looked at him and gestured that he should shut his mouth or else.

Martin said no and rushed to the truck to check on Chinedu. When he approached the truck he noticed another man sitting at the back. Chinedu was now between them as they sat on the wooden benches the stranger had wisely installed in the belly of the truck.

"You want something?" the most ferocious looking of the men inquired.

Martin shook his head to the contrary and watched them drive off with Chinedu.

Later when he relayed the story to Bessem, she said Chinedu might just like him better than the cousin and that was that. But Martin was not so sure. There was something uncomfortable about the men who had come along with Chinedu's cousin. Martin wondered why so many of them had to come along to claim one child. Why? The more he thought about it the more he became confused. But what could he do? He was not even a relative, so why should he really care. He pushed the problem aside and concentrated on his life.

Months later the boy ran all the way from Ekondo Titi, a neighbouring town where they had kept him hostage, all the way to Martin's house to tell him the good news. His cousin was not a good person, he blurted out as soon as he could catch his breath. Martin was sitting on the veranda listening to the story. As Chinedu narrated, Martin kept exclaiming. This attracted the neighbours and soon there was a large crowd in front of Martin's house. Chinedu told them about the man's thriving business. They were impressed.

"I knew it! A Big man!" one neighbour conjectured.

"No, sah, na bad man."

Martin got up from the concrete veranda and dragged the boy into the parlour.

"Why do you say such things about people who want to help you, na Chinedu?"

Chinedu apologized but insisted that the man was not a good person. His big cousin, he added, was not a real Ibo man and had been arrested by the marines for stealing orphans!

"Massa Martin, ah be know; ah be try for tell you. We no bi bad people like you say. We no di chop dog; we no di chop pussy. My papa cousin di do all that. Massa, thank God marines don catcham!" He finally stopped to catch his breath.

Martin could not believe what he was hearing. That evening he ran to the gendarmes to verify the story and they said it was all true. The man picked up these children and used them on his cassava farms. Some he sent to steal from neighbours and retailed the stolen goods in his stores. Martin now believed Chinedu.

"Massa, my Papa die for my eyes. My Mami take me and we run but canoe be too flop so my Mami send me make ah come first." He sighed. "My Mami go come soon, ah know."

"So what am I going to do now?" Martin wondered out loud. "What if your mother never shows up?"

"Eh, Massa?"

"Ah say, wetin ah go do with you now?"

Chinedu smiled broadly. "Ah go be your boy boy. Ah go do any ting for you, Massa. Ah go wash your clothes; ah go cook for you; ah go wash your house; ah go broke firewood for you."

He stopped and stared at his Master's uncertain face. "Massa, ah beg you; I no go chop plenty again; if you like, ah go starve myself."

"Okay, so you will be my house boy then but no chop plenty, you hear?"

"Yes, Massa."

"I don't have much food myself, so don't eat too much again, you hear?"

"Yes, Massa."

"Good. Ah no get plenty food to feed you."

And just like that Martin became a kind of Big man in his own right and that brought him back to what he had long overlooked – becoming a member of the staff club. He was a Big man too, was he not? But Zacharias would still not say either yes or no to him and that hurt Martin so much that he avoided his friend for one whole week. He tried once more through John to no avail. He decided to do something that would make them recognize that he truly had the potential to become a Big man. He decided to get married — not to Magda; not to Joanna. He later told his friends that he married a "pure" girl. He had carefully gone home to his village of origin and handpicked her among the dozens of virgins his relatives had paraded in front of him. She was a primary school dropout but a very pretty one and better yet quite trainable in the ways of the Europeans.

Chapter Eight

He took a loan from the local credit union and had the wedding of the year in the staff club. He had carefully blackmailed his two friends by hinting to them that if he did not use their club for the ceremony, they would not be invited. And of course, that would have shown the public that they were not good enough for Martin's new style. With his bride in white lace and veil and beaded satin ivory purse generously donated by the doctor's wife, they made a grand entrance into the new exclusive club. A train of bridesmaids sprinkled rice as the couple entered the club. Martin and his new bride felt like rich people. Martin, himself, was very impressed with the festivity. Only the best company employees were there. The Black supervisor who had just recently been appointed office manager sat next to the doctor at the high table with roasted chicken and goat meat loaded in huge enamel bowls waiting, and a cake baked by the doctor's cook on the side table. He spent the entire evening trying to converse with the doctor and the man kept nodding in agreement or shaking his head in disagreement but never a word from his mouth. Half an hour later the doctor left and all the Black dignitaries relaxed. The office manager opened the floor, made endless speeches and promised to invite Martin and his bride over to "his club" and eventually to his new house next to Mr. Fox's. Everyone cheered. It was indeed a wonderful wedding present and not long after that he requested a song for the groom and bride to dance. "There's no condition permanent in this world... You can be a rich man today and tomorrow you become poor; you can be a poor man today and tomorrow you become rich;" the music played on with

Martin beaming throughout. How true the lyrics sounded and he too would be Big someday; if not for himself, at least for his bride's sake. He beamed and looked down at his smiling, young, innocent bride. She was gorgeous. He was pleased.

News spread across the estate that Martin Tebi's wedding was the best they had ever seen. A week later he became the first category 5 employee to become a member of the newly established staff club. He liked that so much and never failed to throw his weight around like the real Big men did – buying drinks for others and waiting for people to acknowledge him. He explained to his wife that he was now a "Staff" in his own right and did not need to wait for his friends to invite him anymore to their club. It was wonderful. But his glory did not last long as Zacharias was suddenly promoted to the rank of a supervisor with several staff under his control. Much to Martin's dismay this promotion came with a self-contained house and a brand new Honda! Zacharias was fast on his way to become a black European right under Martin's nose. This hurt so badly; Martin avoided his friend like a plague for an entire week. Several weeks later he was still unable to congratulate his friend. The thought of his friend being a Big man nauseated him and he was glad to learn that Puis too had refused to acknowledge this milestone in their friend's career. Then Martin received a tip that Isaac was being considered for something big as well. "Weh!" he exclaimed on hearing the news. He could not understand how this came about. Why were they having such luck with him having none? Was he not a hard worker too? When would his own fortune shine again na? These thoughts bombarded him as he wondered about his future with the company, waiting to see how things would turn up.

Meanwhile, as he waited to see he tried to drown down his misery in beer but the beer tasted funny that particular day. He bought meat and asked his wife to fry it for him but that also tasted funny. "Weh!" he exclaimed again feeling sorry for himself. He felt extremely sorry for himself moping around all day and wondering when it would be his turn to celebrate something really big. His wife brought him a plate of fried fish. He asked her to take it away. He was not in the mood. He was still in this state of mind when it occurred to him that only one person could make him feel good once more and that was his friend, Puis! What a brilliant idea! The bottle of beer he had stored under some bitter leaves shade to keep cool became handy as he gulped it down with renewed relish. This time it tasted so delicious that he asked his wife to bring back the plates of fried meat and fish. She came running in with two plates and placed them in front of him. He smiled and ate every morsel of grain that accompanied the generous servings of meat without a word.

That evening forgetting their squabble with Puis he visited his friend. The moment he arrived he regretted it right away.

"Na wetin you want now, Martin?"

"Is that your greeting? Can't I miss my friend?"

"I say, what do you really want?"

"What is all this all of a sudden? Must I want something in order to visit you?"

Puis sighed and made room for him on the mat he had placed on the veranda in front of his house. "I thought you came here to laugh at me again."

Martin cleared his throat. "Why would I do that? Am I better?" He looked away. Puis was now interested in whatever news Martin had come to share with him.

"You too feel the pain?" He cupped his chin. "I thought I was the only one who felt the pain. First, Zacharias, then now Isaac?"

"You forget John?"

"Oh, that one was already a Big man before they even made him one. But these two moogus now, how did they become Big? Eh, Boh?"

Martin remained silent.

"Not fair at all!"

"Puis, true; not fair." Martin clapped his hand in wonderment and looked at his friend one more time. The more he looked at Puis the more he became depressed. He did not want to feel sorry for himself anymore, so he bade his friend goodbye and left in a hurry.

The following morning there was commotion on the estate. Someone had scribbled a nasty lyric about the Europeans on one of the buildings, John relayed to Martin. The research night watch man said he saw someone crawling out of there but did not know who it was because the person looked like a "European" in the dark. The moment he said that he was sacked at once and replaced with a new recruit. No one knew who had the courage to insult the white managers like that. Even Martin wondered who would have the gall to do such a thing. The search for the culprit intensified and they finally rallied all the research workers who could read and write for questioning. All four of them including Puis took turns explaining their whereabouts to their boss. After hearing their testimonies the white boss crossed Puis off the list saying he was too feeble-minded to orchestrate such a scheme. Isaac was now the target. He was brought in for questioning several times; interviewed by all the white dignitaries on the estate and his answer was the same. He knew nothing about the graffiti. Finally, they took his word for it and let him go, but the relationship between him and the manager was no longer the same. The man was now constantly suspicious of his local assistant to the point where he began taking his dog along with him wherever he went even to the office. And Isaac was disappointed with this lack of faith in him as a human being and as a loyal employee. He wrote a letter apologizing to the Research manager on the culprit's behalf and begged him to forgive all the ungrateful workers under his wing.

This resolved nothing. When he remembered the hand-me-down clothes and house ware that the manager had given him in the past and would have continued to give him if not of the stupid mess — stuff that could not be found anywhere in the country, he went to the office bathroom and wept long and hard in there. Who would do such a thing to him like this? He mumbled repeatedly. Who hated him so much to the point whereby the person was willing to put a wedge between him and his kind white boss? And why? He blew his nostrils and cried some more. Why were black people so jealous? He muttered to himself with tears shamelessly pouring down his puffy cheeks as though he were a starving child.

Martin wondered about this too but had his suspicions of who the person could be. He kept this to himself and continued working as hard as he could to get the attention of the white doctor in the hospital and life went on. It was not his place to tell Isaac who the possible suspect was. He felt if Isaac had enough sense, he would be able to tell who amongst his friends and co-workers hated him that much. Martin shrugged this thought away and worked harder than ever to win the respect of his own bosses. They were many and he knew they were all watching him including the doctor. He attended to patients diligently administering injections, checking medical charts, giving pills to those in need, explaining case histories to the nurse-in-charge and taking notes from his superiors whenever he erred. At times, he didn't mind running errands for the registered nurses and the medical superintendent. He was ready to be a Big man like his friends were already becoming and would do anything to expedite the process in the hospital. The doctor was impressed by this new attitude; so were the other important hospital staff. But life just went on as usual with none of them promising him greater things in the future as he had hoped.

A few weeks passed by before he heard again from Puis. His friend confided in him that he was happy once more.

Martin did not bother to ask why. These days he remained focused making sure his wife gained enough weight to earn the respectability she deserved as the spouse of a prospective Big man. As he desired, she did gain weight, growing thicker and thicker along the waist line and around the buttocks, and looking plump and fresh. Martin was proud of his beautiful angel and bought her the kind of wrapper that he saw the Black manager's wife tying, only it cost him half a month's salary. He did not care. She too must have good quality loincloth to grace her well-formed bottom. Without any question the fabric must be imported from Europe somewhere. He didn't care where exactly as long as it wasn't from continental Africa, He would take her to their club and insist that the club manager put just the kind of music that he and his wife could waltz to. In his mind they would waltz gracefully across the tiled dancing floor with him whispering in her eyes to "quick, quick, slow; and slow, slow, quick" to the soothing melody just the way he had taught her to do. And each time the music ended the crowd of people in there would applaud and offer them drinks. But each time, Martin would refuse politely, saying he could take care of his young wife just fine. When he said this she would smile and follow her important husband to a nice corner of the room and wait for the next move.

Dancing became their favourite pastime as they spent Sunday evenings in the staff club weekend after weekend until the day that the Europeans introduced a new pastime – movies! Martin was disappointed at first when the Estate Guard announced one day that "Order say, cinema shows tonight." Of course, who could dare to defy what the powers- that- be had so graciously ordered. He knew he had to contend with this new form of recreation like every other company employee. And so the movies came causing frenzy all over the place reminding Martin and his friends once more of their ranks within the company.

The first time a film was shown workers were so happy that for a whole month that was all everyone talked about. As Martin and his friends would discuss while playing their game of draughts, "Actor caught that girl like this and took her away on his horse. And then this beautiful Indian girl will start singing 'Piya, Piya, Piya'..." one of them would mimic the actions of the stars in the movie as he recaptured the plot, recapturing each scene over and over again.

"Ah, ah Martin, that is not how it happened. The girl was an imitation white girl and she was not the one singing. I don't think it was 'piya, piya, piya' at all. It was a nicer Indian song; indeed, some fine Indian tune was the one."

"Zacharias, what did I say na? But she is beautiful na? Imitation white girl or not!"

They would all burst out laughing. Each time it was the same conversation. Then Martin noticed that every Sunday before going to church his wife would adorn her forehead with an "Indian mark." She looked stunning with the mark so much that he would start humming one of the songs from the movies they watched. His beautiful imitation Indian girl!

Life was good, so Mrs. Tebi told him one night after a good meal but Martin thought it could be better and should be better. But how? Surely, not when he had heard the rumour that the company had employed their first set of secondary school graduates. That was not good, he told himself. When he consulted with John, his friend advised him to work harder and get promoted quickly before the real "book people" started joining the company. How would they be able to compete with employees with more education than them? Martin was a bit disturbed by this information. So work hard, Martin did. He worked harder than before and earned one medal after another for diligence on Labour day after Labour day. They commended him for his efforts and finally one day when he could take it no more the hospital superintendent told him the truth, Martin could not be promoted to the rank of a nurse because only officially trained staff are reserved that privilege! This was a shock to Martin. He carried on: "Martin, you see, that is why nobody on this estate can joke with us. We have sense, skills, and diplomas from Ibadan. Where is your own professional certificate?"

"For my box, sir."

"No, no, no, Martin. Not Standard six Certificate! Post primary school certificate." He waited. Martin remained quiet. "You see, you should have remained in the fields!"

"Sir, but I will like to be a nurse, not a field worker," he argued stubbornly.

"You will never be one! Now get out of my office."

Martin walked away slowly until he found himself in a bathroom where he could cry freely. He cried there all alone and wondered what he had done wrong to deserve such a stagnation in his career. He should have just braved it and stayed in the fields like many had advised him before. After reflecting on his life in there for a good half an hour, he went to the Dispenser and asked him for magnesium trisilicate complaining of stomach aches and constant headache. The man obliged adding aspirin and phenegan to the mix. Martin was glad.

When he arrived home he took his tablets and slept well. By the time he got up he already had an idea of how to handle the situation. A week later he put his plan into action. He became a "doctor" in his own right just like that! On his off days he carried a huge plastic first aid kit he had quietly borrowed from the hospital and headed to neighbouring villages to consult. And the peasants came in droves paying first before the "doctor" would tell them what was wrong and prescribed something. One injection here, nine tablets for three days, a teaspoon of antipar, a bottle of notozen and so on. So in this new world he had become a doctor feared and revered. He loved it and carried on like this for years before giving up when an unsterilized syringe he had used on several of his village patients caused complications that needed to be addressed only in a hospital. Then the real doctor took charge. He got so mad that he ordered every hospital worker's house to be searched for evidence. His orders were carried out immediately and Martin and Mr. Okon were rounded up for questioning. Mr. Okon laughed and told them bluntly that he would never have been that stupid. Thereafter all attention turned to Martin.

"Now, Martin Tebee," the doctor began, "why do you have all these supplies in your house?"

Martin looked from doctor to the superintendent sitting next to him. The black man looked more ferocious than the white man who was his boss. It was time to own up, Martin decided.

"Please, sir, Chinedu and my wife are always sick, that's why."

The doctor looked at the superintendent uncertainly with deep concern in his eyes before leaving the office. The superintendent knew what he had to do right away nodding in the doctor's direction.

"Yes, Sir. We will look into the bottom of this problem."

Martin observed the doctor walk unsteadily out of there leaving him behind to negotiate his fate with the next Big man in-charge of little people like him.

The superintendent dragged his chair closer and eyed at Martin sternly.

"You see, Martin, you can fool the Europeans, but you cannot fool me, eh?"

"Yes, sir."

"Good. So now tell me the truth why you opened a clandestine clinic in Bekora?"

Martin broke down and knelt on the floor. "Oga, please, I meant no harm. I just needed more money."

The Black boss laughed, "and so you became a thief and a doctor?" He pulled his chair away from Martin and leaned back for more comfort.

"Wait a minute," he stared down at the culprit again. "You almost became a murderer too, you know, eh, Martin? And you think you can be a real nurse?"

"Sir, please, forgive me. My patients like me and treated me like a doctor. Oga, you understand na?" Martin added.

The medical superintendent laughed curtly and became serious again. "I don't understand."

"Please, sir, don't sack me."

The medical superintendent's softened up. "So this is about you being a Big man? A Big doctor as you say, eh? And not really about money?"

Martin started to nod in agreement but changed his mind.

"Sir, and for money too."

"I thought you said it was about you being a Big man, a medical doctor. That was not it?"

"I did, sir. Big man with money is better."

The medical superintendent relaxed a little before leaning into his chair again. He felt tired suddenly and let his face droop. He looked depressed and unsure as to how to proceed with the case. What was he going to do to an employee who violated the basic hospital code? He thought about the issue some more and stood up and began pacing the office. On his way back to his seat after pacing a couple of times he paused and stared at Martin.

"You are a thief and a semi murderer."

"I know that now, sir," Martin admitted. "But please, sir, I am not a bad person. Forgive me, I beg of you."

"You do?"

He nodded. The medical superintendent sat down and pulled out a ledger from one of his drawers.

"Please, Oga, excuse me. I will not do it again. I have learned my lesson." Martin begged, his tears pouring like those of a child. The Black boss had seen enough. He returned the ledger and got up to leave without resolving the issue.

"Wait, sir; what of Mr. Okon? He too has a clandestine clinic? What is this I am hearing? That my hospital is packed with thieves and potential murderers? Eh? Martin, up at once and go call Mr. Okon."

The younger man dried his tears and dashed out to get Mr. Okon.

"What have I done now?" Mr. Okon inquired as soon as he entered the office.

"Sit down and I will explain."

"No, you explain while I am still standing. What have I done? I told you I was not the one and the European believed me, why can't you believe me? Eh?"

"Sit down, now, Mr. Okon!"

"Okay, don't you shout at me; I am not a small boy, you know." He snatched a chair and sneered at Martin. "Where you come from sef for compare yourself with me, you this Martin?"

"Martin, step out for a minute let me discuss something with Okon."

"Okay, sir." Martin went and waited in the hall.

"I did not open a clinic in Bekora!" Mr. Okon insisted.

"I know, but who is talking about Bekora? How about the other villages?"

Mr. Okon looked at the Black hospital boss with contempt and refused to answer the question.

"Okay, you leave me no choice. I will suspend you then for two days."

Mr. Okon stood up and stared down at the man who had the gall to say such rubbish to him.

"You cannot do that to me; after all, I have the same experience like you!" He wagged his index finger at the boss, "and don't you ever try that again, you hear, Jacob? The only reason you are my boss is because you are from this stupid country."

"Okon, listen."

"No, I will not listen. Were we not classmates once? Eh? I will not listen to any rubbish that comes out of your mouth!" He stormed out of there banging the door behind him almost running into Martin, who had been leaning against the door to eavesdrop on the ground.

"You are such a stupid Cameroonian man, you dis Martin, not even having the good sense to sterilize syringes!bGet out before I kill you."

The younger man got out of his way just in time.

"Martin?"

"Sir."

"Come on in now."

He rushed back in and waited.

The medical superintendent shuffled some papers and placed in a drawer. "That was my report on you and Mr. Okon. You are suspended for one week, you hear?"

Martin nodded and thanked the Black boss. That was a close call. He ran out of there without looking back. When he found Mr. Okon again the man was rambling in his dialect.

"You dis stupid boy, you do not follow me again, you hear?" His accent got thicker.

Martin steered clear of him and waited for the news of the event to start spreading. It did as always but he was ready for it.

Every day thereafter he searched for an appropriate way to make peace with Mr. Okon. But each time Mr. Okon would brush him aside making a sign in the air to indicate that Martin was a traitor. Martin felt sad about this. He did not like to be perceived as a traitor, for he believed in his heart that he was not a bad person. One evening when his shift was over he waited for Mr. Okon on the veranda. The older man ignored him as he had been doing since the clinic fiasco.

"Etey, you too cannot forgive someone?" he shouted as the man walked by without acknowledging him. Martin dusted the back of his trousers and followed Mr, Okon to his house pleading for forgiveness. As Mr. Okon set one foot on the bottom step to open his front door, he turned around and stared hard at Martin.

"You want forgiveness? Okay, I forgive you. Now leave me alone."

"Thank you, Etey."

"Yes, you go, go, go and let me have my peace in this your God forsaken country." He shooed him away like a chicken. Martin did not mind. He returned home feeling less burdened than before. The next morning, Mr, Okon stopped by Martin's and dropped off something.

"You remind me of my small brother back home; foolish, foolish boy just like you!"

Martin did not understand what the older man meant. So he stood on the veranda and waited for Mr. Okon to explain more.

"You so, if you dare do what you did to me in the hospital again, you will be in trouble. Big, big trouble. I mean it." Mr. Okon scratched his scalp. "Just ask my foolish, small brother who is like you."

He turned around to leave. "Take this envelope and don't forget to greet your madam for me."

Martin watched the man walk away with gentle strides in harmony to the tune he was whistling. When Mr. Okon was no longer in sight Martin looked at the envelope in his hand. He noticed it was not sealed, so he quickly opened it to see what was inside. There was a piece of paper in there and nothing else. Martin pulled it out at once and read what was written on the piece of paper aloud. He hissed a laugh and read it again. It was an address. This puzzled him further. He turned the paper over but there was nothing else written on it. He examined the back of the envelope for the name of an addressee. There was none to be found. Hmm! He inserted the paper back into the envelope and sighed.

Mr. Okon disappeared and a month later he reappeared. He still would not explain the envelope. A few months later Martin learned that Mr. Okon had tendered in his letter of resignation, collected his benefits and disappeared. It happened so fast no one knew the details or what had prompted this action. Martin felt bad about this as he remembered what he had told the Black boss about Mr. Okon. Some said he had left the country; others speculated that he was working for a rival company in a different part of the country. Still others believed he might be practicing medicine in one of the interior villages. Regardless of what they thought no one knew for sure what had happened to Mr. Okon, including Martin. But it was as though Mr. Okon had set the pace, for other foreigners followed suit. Resignation letters after resignation letters were handed in and stopped only when the marines began retrieving headless bodies of former employees in the creeks.

No one knew what was happening anymore, even though the company sent out a series of queries to the different heads of division as well as the government officials in that area. No one was able to shed more light into the situation until one day the marine search team found what they thought was another lifeless body floating along the shores of the Ndian river. Miraculously, the head was still attached to the rest of the body and the person though seriously injured was still breathing, albeit with difficulty, but still breathing nonetheless. When the marines pulled him out of the water, they made a startling discovery that he was the estate manager's former washer man. They rushed him to the hospital right away and Martin's crew took over working diligently night and day to restore his health. Gradually, he responded to treatment and was able to explain what had happened to him, but no one was ready for what he had to say.

"Please sah, I saw the cut necks."

"You saw what?" The doctor was puzzled by this.

"Think again, Joseph; who did this to you?" The estate manager who had visited him a couple of times as he wrestled with his life added.

"I no see them; masks cover deir face."

"But you just said..." the doctor gave up.

"You two take care of him then." His job there was done as he handed over the investigation to the estate manager and his team.

Joseph later narrated the story explaining that although he did not see their faces, he recognized the voices behind the mask. The Marines who had recovered his almost lifeless body and the company officials doubted his story at first, but when he started giving names they took him seriously. He spewed out the names without holding back. There were ten names altogether carefully written down by the estate manager's ledger clerk.

Panic gripped the entire estate to imagine some of their former colleagues had master-minded all the killings. But for what, many asked? For the benefits, the former washer man had said. Hmmm! All these happenings in the area freaked Martin out. For a week he dreamt that someone came into his house one day and tried to cut his head off. When he shared this dream with his friends they told him to snap off it. He pretended but the dream persisted and that was when he contemplated sharing them with someone else who might actually listen and give him sound advice, but there was no such person around him who would not make fun of him. He missed Mr. Okon and began toying with the idea of sending a letter to the mysterious address he had found in the envelope. He reflected about it several times and each time he would decide against such a letter. But one day, he could no longer resist the urge to write. He convinced himself that it was worth trying to see if it was an actual address or not. So he wrote a long letter sharing all that had happened on the estate since Mr. Okon left. He paused for a moment to ponder whether it was wise to write about all the terrible dreams he had been having. Yes, it was, he convinced himself. Before ending the long letter he apologized again and begged for forgiveness one more time reminding Mr. Okon that a brother was always a brother no matter how foolish he was. So he should not forget about him too since he reminded him so much of his foolish brother. This brought a smile to Martin's lips. Before sealing the envelope he indicated that he would not mind the older man sharing his interpretations of the dreams he had been having. The letter was long, informative and sweet. The older man replied promptly stating it was all the deeds they hushed over there at the plantation that was coming back to haunt Martin. Martin found the letter mysterious. Was it a cryptic message? If so, what exactly was the Etey himself trying to tell him. For fear of been punished he could not discuss the contents of the letter with any of his hospital colleagues. Neither could he discuss it with any of his friends. He wrote another one and the Etey replied right away including pictures of his new thriving clinic. In one picture, he had his company overalls on with the name tag and all. Martin was nervous about this. In another, he stood next to a former company yardman. He labelled the picture "assistant doctor Okon and hospital staff." Martin looked closely at another one with all four of Mr. Okon's staff. He could recognize one former ward servant. They stood in front of Mr. Okon's "Good Will Clinic!" Martin was impressed. He decided to send a picture of his family to Mr. Okon. He waited for more letters and nothing came back. After a while he forgot about Mr. Okon just like that and concealed the original envelope that held the address the older man had slipped into his hands before leaving, along with the letters he had received from him in his suitcase.

Chapter Nine

"Martin, have you heard the news?" Puis shouted late one afternoon kicking the door to his bedroom open. "Ah, Missus, I did not know that you were in there with your Oga-oh." He apologized and went on, "Martin big, big news!" He pushed the couple over to one side of the bed and created space for himself close to the edge to plant his skinny buttocks.

"Yes, what is it this time, Puis?"

Puis ignored him and concentrated on making himself comfortable.

"Puis, am I not talking to you?" Martin sat up adjusting the covers over his wife. "Or have you come this time to drive me away from my own house too?"

"No, no, no. Ah, ah, Boh, can't you forget that silly joke." He became serious again. "And by the way, you people have forgotten to take the draught board from my house."

"I thought John took it away."

"Which John? The baggar did not. Anyway, now that you have mentioned him... Boh, Martin, do you know that he has just been made a manager? Can you imagine our own friend a Big, Black Whiteman?"

Martin sat up fully scrubbing his eyes. "Weh! What kind of bad luck do I have so-eh?"

"That is not all. He will have cooks, yardmen, stewards and will be drinking tomato juice, guava juice, cow juice, goat juice and all that white man juice weh they all drink in that their European quarters!"

Martin was dumbfounded. It was official; his own bad luck was more than that of any other employee on the estate.

"Martin, Martin?" Puis shook his friend on the arm. "Are you with me? Red Volkswagen and driver too. Boh do you know that he was the only one among us who did not really have a Standard 6 certificate? A Standard 5 drop out bastard!"

"Weh! Weh! Weh!" Martin jumped out of his bed and hurriedly put on his khaki trousers to cover his blue polo underwear. "You say what, Puis? That John is what now?"

"Big man! He will be playing golf, riding horses and swimming with Europeans in the same pool with his dirt rubbing off their white flesh." Puis chuckled. "You know something; and he will be calling us 'young chaps' through a hole. Do you know that, that is what the first Black manager does?"

"I can't believe it. But he was right all along. 'Stay in the field,' he had said 'and you'll be a Big man!' But poor me, I could not stand the mud, the rain, the beatings, the garri drinking day-in, day-out! Weh!"

Puis was shocked. "You left because of garri drinking? Bush man. Is that not what you do in your own house now?"

"You see me drinking garri every day? Go sleep."

"No, no, no! Anyway, you complain; what about Isaac? What about Zacharias? Are they not Big men too? Did they go to the field? Look at me here." He sighed and covered his face in his hands. "I have tried everything. But . . ." his voice faltered.

"I know what you mean. It's destiny."

"No, it is not; it is just pure bad luck." He shook his head pitifully. "Do you know that my mother always said I was a bad luck child because I came out feet first?" He smiled. "But my Pa always said I had special powers. Special powers my foot! I have waited and waited and not seen these powers..." His voice faltered again.

Someone sighed.

"Missus? Oh my God, your woman has seen me almost cry, Martin? Weh! Am I a man anymore?" He got up and dragged himself to the parlour.

"Anastasia?"

"Sah."

Mrs. Tebi joined them in the parlour.

"Can you make us something to fill our stomachs?"

She looked at Puis, then back at her husband and walked out of the room. Moments later they heard her screaming for Chinedu.

"Puis, true, true, what do you think is happening?"

"Like what?" He leaned back on his seat. Martin was surprised.

"What do you mean 'like what?' You and I becoming Big men na?"

Puis did not respond.

"Okay. Are you not afraid just a little bit?"

Puis nodded.

"I don't know anymore," Martin sighed. "I feel like I just wasted my time climbing that truck that day. Running and going to a strange place like a Bororo cow only to come here and mark time. I feel so." He stood up to check on his wife and Chinedu. When he returned he was more relaxed. "Well, I have enjoyed life a bit; I cannot deny that fact. See my small house!"

"Yes, indeed." Puis concurred, swallowing spit as he repressed something within him. "Yes, indeed," he said again burying his face in his lap. Envy was choking him as he thought about Martin and the others in clubs that he could never be a member of. There were days he had longed to taste beer that was served in the Staff club just to compare the taste with the one served in his own club – the bed bug club! Not a chance. He remembered being shoved out of the gate by a gateman who had later confessed to him in their bed bug club over a beer that it was Mr. Zacharias who had ordered him to "kick out people of your type." Puis remembered this all too well. He had simply retaliated by sending a child to plant excreta wrapped in plantain leaves at Zacharias' door step. He smiled at the thought. They had almost eaten his shit. He burst out laughing.

"Puis, are you alright?"

"No, Martin. Just something funny weh ah remember. He dismissed the memory of Zacharias and sat up right. "Is the food coming or not?"

"Let me check again." Martin went out and came back. "The Missus is still working on it. May be a game of draught while we wait. Chinedu!"

The boy came running from the kitchen where he was helping Mrs. Tebi. Martin sent him off to Puis' house to get the game.

That evening they played four matches and Martin won every single one of them. Tired of losing again, Puis finished his beer and left more dejected than before. He came over a couple more times and each time he lost. Finally, he declared to his friend that he did not like the game. Instead he would like to know how to play tennis. Martin looked him straight in the eye and told him he was not willing to teach him. Puis returned home that day not sure of how to punish Martin. What kind of a friend would say no to a friend, he asked his wife. She said only bad friends say "no" to real friends and that was that. Puis boycotted Martin's house for a while thereafter to deal with the pain that accompanied such a betrayal by one's friend.

But then Anastasia Tebi got pregnant and had the baby as if women just went to the market and picked them up. No spitting during the nine months duration; no vomiting, no grumpiness, and not a tear came out of her eyes as she pushed the tiny baby girl out on the labour bed. The midwives were amazed but impressed. They treated her with the utmost care. She was a special woman. Three times a day, a trained staff, not a ward servant or a dresser, would give this young mother a bath in a special enamel basin reserved only for the wives of Black managers. Why were they treating her thus? Puis wondered. Martin explained that she was the first woman who had delivered there without using profanity when pushing out her child. Martin was therefore a hero. He told everyone that his wife's dignified behaviour was a result of good training from him. He had actually drilled her on the whole act of pushing out babies without feeling the pain. People listened and laughed at the stupid bragger. A week later when Anastasia left the hospital the entire female medical staff escorted her home. Martin celebrated his first born in style, passing out rounds of drinks and asking women to serve more porridge plantains with stockfish. He was a proud papa and husband to a woman who was tough. As people poured in daily to congratulate him, he ordered Chinedu to borrow more chairs from the neighbours Martin was a Papa now. He felt it, liked it, and threw his weight around like a real Big man. And the celebration went on for one whole week. By the end of that week he was one poor man. He searched his pockets for loose coins but could find nothing so he turned to wild cassava and kene kene soup to feed his nursing wife. She ate this without complaint. He was indeed a lucky man!

The seasons changed, and the company expanded with more employees pouring in like nothing Martin had seen before. More palm nurseries were opened and new seedlings planted and new fields developed, but Martin remained a Sick Attendant. Two areas of his life expanded though: his belly and his family. By the time he was middle aged Martin had a room packed with lots and lots of children. One day as he counted some change to buy something to feed them he admitted it was time he took stock of his life again.

He was frightened when he actually did this realizing that he was almost running out of time to become a Big man. Young recruits were now bossing him left and right and his friends were being promoted left and right as well. It was not fair. And then one day they brought a 'freshly minted' nurse from a prestigious nursing school to boss Martin around. He refused to take orders from her. She reported him to the doctor who wrote a warning and put it in Martin's records. Martin obeyed thereafter until the day he found her struggling to get penicillin into a syringe and poked her hand instead. Martin lost respect for her again. She threatened to take him up and he dared her warning that he too would take her up for incompetence. The matter died there.

Life was changing faster than he could imagine. It seemed like whenever he woke up in the morning there was a new employee. This would have been a good thing but for the fact that they were all more educated than him and always half his age. He sighed several times and wondered why life could not just stop for one moment and let him at least figure out what he needed to do to get a *good* promotion like the others. But this was not so. Puis kept complaining too. That was when Martin finally acknowledged that they had missed the boat.

"So?" Puis posed one fine day.

"You still have a chance, Puis. As for me, what are my chances here with all these diploma dunces?"

"Boh, you really think so?"

"But of course. All you need to do is learn the difference between Dura, Tenera, and Pesifera, not so? Are these not the kind of palm nuts we produce on this estate?"

Puis sighed and punched him in the face. "You are really a bush thing. You think I do not know the difference? Eh? Look at a man who cannot convince people to make him a real nurse come and talk rubbish to me about palm nuts."

Martin could not understand. He thought it was really easier for Puis to pass the exam and get out of the rot instead of remaining bitter forever and ever. He shrugged his shoulders and forgot about his friend for that moment. That evening at his place, he beat Puis at the draught game again.

"See?"

"See what? You think because I lose at this game I am stupid?"

"I did not say so. I am saying you have a chance to move up. Your work no need book sense. All it needs is experience sense! Go observe those seedlings at the nurseries and go pass the exam, you lazy man."

Puis had had it. He stood up, dusted the back of his trousers and left without saying bye.

When Puis went to the office the following day, as if fate wanted to punish him further he ran into some newly employed college students. He greeted them and headed to the back room to get a ledger for his day's task. One followed him in there. Puis waited for him to say something and he did.

"Mr. Puis, are you the one they say does not know the difference between Tenera and Dura?"

Puis ignored the remark and headed back to his desk to begin work. The trouble maker followed him over there. "Are you?" He was already laughing so hard tears were pouring out of the corner of his eyes. "How can you not even know that? Don't you eat palm nut?" He laughed out loud again. Puis took a look at a boy who was almost his son's age and ground his teeth. The young employee disappeared only to reappear with more tears streaming down his cheeks with Isaac sharing his mirth. Puis was more than embarrassed. He was infuriated, embarrassed, and sad – all at once! The next time around he passed the bar exam with flying colours and was promoted instantly to category 5, which came with lots of perks as well. He had finally made it somewhat! When his rejoicing was over he spotted Isaac's motorcycle parked by the staff club and his anger returned. Puis slashed the tires and went back to celebrate some more. He gave everyone a round of drinks. He was a Big man too.

Isaac came in complaining that someone had vandalized his Honda. Puis drank some more ordering a second round to those willing to drink some more.

"Boh, do you want to kill yourself?" Martin asked him. Puis turned to him and snorted.

"Okay-oh; I am just worried that you are drinking too much."

Puis put down his bottle of schnapps and turned around to face his friend. "Are you saying that I cannot afford it?"

Martin backed out of the bar and headed elsewhere in the club. Puis followed him with a pen knife in his hand this time.

"Isaac, are you saying that I am not a Big man?"

Martin looked at him funny. "Boh, it is me, Martin."

Puis swung the hand with the knife in the air. "Imitation Whiteman, you think you are better than me because you sit behind the manager's car? Eh? Look at me!" His voice sounded crazy. "I am now the Chief Ledger Clerk in that research! Isaac, soon I will get your position." He brandished the knife again. Martin and the others restrained him and finally took him home away from the scene.

"Puis?" Martin tried to talk some sense into him. "What is wrong with you? Don't you know that Big men don't disgrace themselves in public?"

"I am a Big man," his speech was slurred at this point as they were dragging him onto his bed.

At work the following morning he was disciplined and warned that if he repeated his actions again Isaac would sack him. Puis' humiliation had come full circle. He went to the bathroom and washed his hands and face thoroughly, looked at himself in the mirror and wept bitterly in there. Why was it so hard to be a Big man-eh? He washed his eyes again and practiced the right smile to take back to the office where the other ledger clerks sat waiting and of course, the college graduate who had taunted him also sat waiting as his immediate boss. Life was truly unfair!

His success made him a better man though and he vowed to remain good unless... So with a little help from Martin he regained his membership into the staff club and life went on as usual. But somehow Martin could no longer enjoy his own life. He was seen less and less at the club now that the Europeans had begun leaving along with their country and classical music. What was the use, he confided in his wife, now mother of several children with a much more expanded waistline that made Martin more proud of his ability to take care of a woman. His lifestyle became very simple: he got up from bed, ate breakfast, went to work and then returned home when it was over. It was always the same. Some days when he was walking along the road, John's red Volkswagen would pass by splashing mud all over his white overalls. Martin would simply turn around and return home to change. He had long concluded that it was the way of the world. Why blame his friend who had hung out there in the fields and taken all the abuse and surely become a Big man?

Life at work became monotonous; life at home was not getting better either with children who were always fighting over food; fighting over where to sleep night after night. What could he really do? Was he such a big failure? Was he worse off than Puis? Yes? No? Why bother anymore. He decided to arrange with a neighbour to let Chinedu sleep over at her place. The neighbour gladly accepted and for a while things seemed to be working all right somewhat until the day that a huge girl who looked like a woman knocked on their door and asked to see Mr. Martin. He could tell she was not a woman yet by the firmness of her body. Martin could still smell trouble. He let her into his parlour and asked right away what she wanted. She looked at him disdainfully and opened her right palm. He did not understand.

"Now, my own money!"

This confused him even further. Anastasia looked at Martin and then at the girl.

"Na your girl friend?" she asked."

He was disappointed in her. He raised his hand as though to spank her but changed his mind. "You are not even ashamed sef. I don't have money to feed you and your battalion, what do you expect me to do with an outside woman?"

She left them there and went about her business. Martin concentrated on the younger woman.

"What did you say?"

"Money, right now."

He sighed and simply handed over a 500 frs note he had in his pocket. She disappeared and he hoped it was forever. But three months later she showed up again this time with a bag dangling from her shoulder and a pair of shoes in her hand. Anastasia just watched her drop her belongings on the floor and sat down on the sofa. Anastasia clapped her hands in wonder and sighed. Whatever it was she knew she had not brought that kind of baggage into her marital home; after all, she had left all her siblings far away in the village. So she wandered away from the scene leaving the younger woman in the parlour idling about as the children played in the yard. When Martin returned from work Anastasia met him on the veranda and opened the door blind for him to see what was waiting in the living room. He was confused again sighing long and loud.

"What do you want in my house again?" He was too exhausted for niceties. When he got no response he sent Chinedu to go look for Mami Trisha. His neighbour came running.

"Martin, what has happened now?"

He showed her the young woman sitting in his parlour. She folded her hands. "Is this why you sent for me? Do you know that I have a pot on the fire?"

"Sit down and cool your temper na. This thing is more than me."

"Okay." Mami Trisha turned to the young woman. "You be who?"

The girl sighed rolling her eyes.

"Martin, you were right to call for me." She fastened her wrapper around her waist and waited for the girl to respond. The girl took her time to utter a word and when she did speak up Mami Trisha left them alone calling Martin a foolish man who fathered children and threw them away, for the girl turned out to be Magda's daughter – all grown-up. Martin was surprised. Had the years flown by so fast? He enquired about the girl's mother's health. But she too had no idea where her mother was. She said she had tracked down her father by some stroke of luck and simply needed a place to stay. Her grandmother was too poor to keep her anymore and her aunt Joanna, now married to a school teacher had too many children of her own to be bothered with them. Martin took all she told them at face value and made room in his already overcrowded house for one more child. It was his lot in life and he would deal with it accordingly, he later explained to his patient and understanding wife.

And it would have worked out well for all of them had Anastasia not noticed months later that the girl was pregnant. Martin hit the roof and asked her to leave his home. She said it was her home too and she was going nowhere. He threatened her and she threatened back so he gave up and felt sorry for himself. Why was his life not turning out the way it should? He asked his wife, who said she had no idea how he imagined his life would be. He was so ashamed of the current state of his life that he withdrew from the club completely. Instead, he was content with watching his children singing and dancing under the moonlit yard night after night. They seemed so happy and so free from problems that it hurt him so badly. Why could he not be as content anymore? He had done the right thing in leaving his people far away up north to come seek out his fortune and this was the most he could get? A Sick Attendant? What was that even? Not a nurse; not a ward servant; just some title that came with a whole lot of responsibilities no one was willing to acknowledge at all in the bloody hospital, he thought. He could still see how they had shepherded them onto that lorry several years ago like a herd of cattle, but his luck perhaps might have run out. Or was it still waiting to be tapped?

Yes, it was, Bessem a trained colleague told him one day. She said the company would be giving exams to people like Martin with experience to give them an opportunity to obtain proper training in a reputable training school and become proper nurses. Martin was glad and his mirth returned. Not even Magda's daughter could steal that moment from him. He re-registered at the club and started drinking beer again. On one of his weekly recreations he spotted Magda's daughter now even larger than he had noticed at home, boasting to a loud crowd that she was carrying Chinedu's child. The crowd went wild when she mimicked how Martin had responded when he and his wife had realized that she was in the family way. They laughed harder watching her wag her finger and then placed her hands akimbo to demonstrate further.

"Mami Belly, so this is what you do when we are not around?" Martin announced his presence feeling humiliated. She ignored him. The people were still laughing with some pulling chairs to sit down for more drama. Martin ignored them. "So it was Chinedu all this while-eh?"

She still would not respond.

"Okay." Martin left her there to finish her story. But later he humbled himself and went to see Zacharias in his office to plead for a job for Chinedu, who had impregnated his daughter. Zacharias said there was little he could really do because the jobs in his office were meant for literate employees and not illiterates like Chinedu. He advised Martin to go see John. Martin thanked his friend a million times for welcoming him into his comfortable office. The following evening, he humbled himself again and paid a visit to his long time friend, John who now lived in the European Quarters. Despite so much barking from the dogs and the howling and snappy comments from the different gatemen that protected the area, Martin found his way right up to John's yard. The last gateman came out at once and told him he was trespassing. But John's wife said it was all right to let Martin on their property. She showed him a seat in one of the living rooms and he sat down and waited for her to say something.

"He is not home you know?" She initiated the conversation as he had expected.

He nodded. "I'll wait." He could smell stewed beef coming from the kitchen and heard the sound of something simmering on the charcoal grill. He licked his lips and waited for the Madam to offer him some kind of store bought snack or drink. Instead, she gave him a tall glass of iced water. He was still grateful. She left him there and disappeared in one of the numerous rooms in the Big house. He waited alone there for hours for his friend to return. When John did return he was surprised to see his old friend sitting in the section of the parlour meant for commoners.

"What can I do for you Martin?" He said casually waiting for Martin to outline the problem. He was a Big man and was accustomed to solving little people's problems. Martin stammered as he explained his family situation to John, who told him not to worry. "We'll see what I can do for you, and your chap, eh?"

"Yes, sir," Martin agreed.

John scratched his head and coughed. He too could smell good food coming from the kitchen. "Have they served you anything?"

"No," Martin hesitated before adding, "sir."

John seemed pleased with himself shouting over the sofa for the steward.

Martin panicked.

"No, sir; I am not really hungry," he lied. John could hear his stomach rolling.

"Okay." He said simply and shouted again to alert the steward they would not be needing anything. Martin's face dropped.

"Obviously the boy cannot read and write, but if I remember well, he is quite industrious," John carried on.

"You know him well na, John?"

John gave Martin a strange look that reminded his friend of his social standing in the company. Martin got the message right away.

"I can arrange something with Max, my former head man. He is a nice chap. I think he'll have something for your boy in that factory of his. Just make sure you tell your boy to meet me tomorrow in front of the factory." He stood up briskly. Martin followed suit thanking him a million times for his friendship. John walked him to the door and shook his hand.

"Next time, just let someone in my home know you are coming or else the dog will bite your behind." He laughed heartily. "It is company policy – no stray campers around our quarters."

"Okay, sir," Martin replied hoping that there would never be a reason for him to visit that Big house again. Once, way out of sight he started cursing the day he was born, the day he joined the company, the day John became his friend. He threw stones in the air as he vented his spleen about the unjust way of life. How could someone not as intelligent as him live like that while he who was the smartest in their batch was grovelling! How was that fair when he worked equally as hard? He could take rubbish from all those Europeans, but from John? No way! He spat on the side of the road and dodged in time from being hit by someone driving a manager's car.

" Black bastard!" he cursed.

He felt a sudden rage and wished John were there for him to punch the smirk off his superior face. Instead, he tossed more stones in the air and watched them land right back on the ground where he had picked them. Tired of doing this, he slowly found his way back home. It was a long walk back as he passed cooks, yardmen, stewards, washer men and gatemen with hostile looks. He told himself repeatedly that he was not afraid, and that he was better than they were, for they were glorified house boys. And so with these words of affirmation he survived his journey back to the camps where he belonged.

Chinedu got the job and a house that went with his rank as a company labourer. He was so pleased that he thanked Mr. Martin one million times too. Martin felt like a Big man. He had also solved a little man's problem. As he helped Chinedu pack his sparse belongings he could not help but sniff the aroma that came from the kitchen. Anastasia was frying a lot of onion with some sardines to throw on some rice for them to eat. The aroma hit the air and Martin became hungry. He hurriedly escorted Chinedu and returned home for his delicious meal. He was the man of the house there and it felt good. He felt so good that he later forced Chinedu to marry Magda's daughter or else he would turn him over to the gendarmes for deportation. And within two weeks of having the first paying job ever in his life Chinedu became a husband and looked forward to becoming a Big man at least to his wife. Meanwhile life at the Tebis went on as always.

Part Two

Chapter Ten

Smoke kept pouring despite the exodus of some key pioneers, for as the company expanded they headed elsewhere to seek more fortunes, better fortunes, or to take on new challenges. Some by choice; others well? No one knew or understood their motivations. They just left without warning, notifying the company only weeks later when they were already settled elsewhere. But the daily grind continued on this estate that Martin Tebi and his four friends had ventured out there not knowing what to expect, and yet hoped for more that life could offer any ambitious young man or young woman. Was it worth it? This was a question that haunted Martin every day. And he was also getting up there in age.

The factory however continued to spew tons and tons of smoke into the clear blue sky — EVERY DAY! The rich aroma of freshly cooked palm fruits would fill the air and mouths would water as workers craved some of these delicious palm nuts to chew on and on and savour its delicate flavour that coated the tip of their tongues. Unable to control this ongoing craving, some would simply go ahead and toss a cooked piece of the finest palm nut into their mouths and sink their teeth into the meat relishing the reddish, greasy juice that spilled from the corners of their mouths. It was delightful. It tasted like nothing they ate at home. Others would simply feed on the fresh kernels, which they watched flying through a separate compartment and heading toward another section of the factory to be converted into kernel oil. And most often for these workers these nuts was lunch as each saved money to send to his village of origin or to raise children they had fathered everywhere and over the years.

The boiler hummed churning the cooked fruits into a massive mess of grease, which came out as sweet tasting palm oil further away in another part of the factory. The company hands had become quite efficient at what they did. And the crops in the fields flourished with larger bunches of palm produce being harvested these days with John just beaming as the real manager in charge. Yes, he was indeed... NOW! And life went on. The factory would chime its hour alerting employees that it was time to get up; it was time to eat; it was time to sleep; it was time to do this and that. It had become so routine that no one cared. They simply abided by what it reminded them to do. Each time it chimed someone sighed somewhere on the estate. What is it that I have to do now? Perhaps a wife who had not fixed lunch for her family would be the anxious one. Perhaps a husband who was not ready to go home and confront his reality would have to budge. Or perhaps it was a European manager not ready to let go of the reigns wondering if his Black subordinates would fare well without his constant guidance. All these notwithstanding, the factory clock had been programmed to chime the right time as the factory spewed more thick smoke into the peaceful sky.

The smoke left a trail of white cloud with patches of gray fumes in its midst; but the real dark smoke sometimes took over making the air heavy and difficult to breathe. It would 'puff and puff' endlessly with little time to pause in synchrony with the boiler that growled as it churned pushing out more fresh hot oil into waiting tankers to be delivered somewhere. That was the reality. Day in, day out, people worked hard to keep this reality going. Black or White, everyone's destiny was linked to the gigantic factory that stood in the middle of the estate surrounded by tall palm trees and badly graded roads. One blunder and Martin and the rest would find themselves hopping back on the truck and heading back up north – only now they would seem like tamed beasts being hurled back home never to return.

But so far nothing had happened to warrant this. For the seasons and years had not altered the works of this graceful building that could be mistaken for a Cathedral from afar. It was massive and majestic and it just stood there harnessing all the energy it could get from the crowd that flocked in, and the machines that propelled it.

Of course, it was busy cooking and pouring oil as skilful hands manipulated black red, green, yellow and even white buttons the pioneers had carefully put in place. It took nonsense from no one, not even its creators. An aerial view captured the image much better as it showed Lobe estate trapped in the middle of a palm island with one impossible building that ruled everyone's life. This aerial view of this thriving community was splendid. Like the board on which Martin and his friends used to play draught one could clearly notice the boundaries and the endless possibilities prevalent within the new and thriving plantation community. If only Martin could see it from far above, his secret drops of fortune would become a heavy down pour that needed a larger vessel to contain. But he was not that visionary.

The thriving community seemed like a paradise with its green grass stretching from one manager's house to another bringing out the unspoiled beauty of the dusty road in contrast to the well kept orchard which was heavy with overripe fruits and the carefully planned residential quarters for the others. Nice house, nice place; okay house, okay place, blending together – rich, poor, stupid, not so stupid – to complete what Lobe estate stood for. The sight was breathtaking with green lawns and tall green luscious palm trees with their thick trunks deeply entrenched in the rich soil and happy children running wildly without a care in the world, including Martin's children. It would make a great painting on the canvas of a skilful artist.

From one angle, one could feel the richness of the land and smell the sweetness of the red palm oil that was being produced daily. The smoke spewed everywhere and the managers would smile and be proud of their hard work and creation. Those who got promoted sooner than they expected were proud as well. But Martin? He had failed the exam to get into nursing school too many times. Only Magda's daughter was bold enough to tell him to his face that his brains were getting old. Martin took these words to heart and wept in the hospital bathroom for one whole week — an hour today, thirty minutes the next day, ten minutes and so on as he pretended constantly to use the water system toilet. Was he really that old? He counted how long he had been employed by the company and realized that Magda's daughter just might have a point. He did not have to agree with her though. So to prove his point he made Anastasia pregnant again. It was a set of twins this time. Martin beamed admitting he still got what it took to make a woman complete. Life was good after all.

The smoke continued filling the air, blending with the clouds whether the old workers were ready to admit the passage of time or not. It did not matter who was manipulating the buttons. And so were the workers' lives. Like Martin, they just kept performing their jobs as best as they had been trained by someone to do so. Only at times they did not really understand why they were doing anything at all, or even why they were there. This usually happened when problems plagued them nonstop. And they would sit quietly on verandas or somewhere public and simply clap their hands in wonder and later confide in loved ones what hard luck they have had all these years. Some, like Martin would exclaim as always: "Which kind bad luck be this-eh!" But like the others he too would always hang in there waiting for that opportunity to move up the chain in command, understanding that it could be a while. Yes, a while. However, like the huge factory that never got tired and didn't have the slightest idea what lay ahead, they performed their chores daily and waited. The factory chimed nine p.m. and it was time for Martin to close his shift and return home to his family. Everything was so carefully planned; so carefully planned that it was hard to notice what seemed out of place. But...?

Chapter Eleven

Many years passed and it finally dawned on Martin Tebi that he would never become a Big man in the hospital, so he stopped taking those qualifying exams and accepted his life. After all, was he not the boss of so many other professionals, right there in the hospital? His responsibilities were clear: consult, prescribe, administer, and return home to the family. He would go to work each morning, write out prescriptions, do this, do that, and give precise instructions to an aide. It was a good routine that boosted his ego. He ordered his aides and ward servants about so much that he sometimes forgot who he was and began addressing them as 'chaps' and 'lads' like the managers did. But when the doctor and the medical superintendent were around he would quickly become wise and take his place in the social ladder that prevailed in that environment. At least, they recognized his years of experience, he consoled himself. And that was what actually mattered – so far.

With his brood of children at school things were becoming even more difficult. No matter what he did his earnings was never enough. Anastasia nagged about that all the time driving him crazy; but when he sought solace in work, he ran into colleagues whose sole goal was to boss him around like a little kid. There was little he could do to remedy the situation, so he humbled himself and asked his wife to help out "somehow" and she agreed. Chinedu taught her how to plant cassava and how to make garri. He taught her how to trade and a year later Anastasia Tebi had a basin of garri and trays of water-foofoo permanently on their veranda selling them. On weekends, his children would carry trays of foodstuff to sell in different parts of the estate and returned home with lots of money. That pleased Martin so much he relaxed a little.

This happiness was short-lived however, for one Sunday Zacharias met him at a football match and told him that it was unbecoming of his family to sell food like common people.

"Boh, I do not understand. The money helps a lot," Martin protested.

"So you want everyone on this estate to know that you are a poor man?"

Martin was unsure about this but he continued to listen.

"Your kids all over the place shouting 'fine garri, fine water foofoo' who is going to promote you? Total disgrace, young fellow."

He could not believe that Zacharias had just referred to him as a "young fellow." Martin laughed. Once upon a time he would have accepted his friend's advice. No more.

"See, Zacharias, you are a Big man now. You cannot understand life." He attempted to be polite.

"No, no, no," Zacharias protested. "Do you think Big people too are free from life's troubles?"

Martin looked at him as if he was being facetious.

"Anyway, how Big am I really?" He added puffing up a bit and eagerly awaiting the cherished words of praise that Martin would generously give. Martin laughed. He understood the routine.

"You are a Big man and you know it. How many supervisors does the company have?" He continued laughing tapping his friend on the shoulders. Zacharias nodded and joined in laughing.

"You people are next in line only to John them."

Zacharias beamed. How true. He knew it was just a matter of time before he would move on up just like their friend, John. He quickly counted the number of possible managerial positions that were open now that most of the

Europeans had left, and noticed there were more than he could have imagined. At this revelation he whistled, for he had never given as much thought to the possibility as he did at that moment. He tapped Martin fondly on the shoulder. "You are a wise man, my friend. A true, true friend."

Encouraged, Martin went on. "True, true, Zacharias I don't know why you have never been made like John yet?"

"No, that would come in good time. Quite soon."

"Eh?" His eyes lit up. "So make ah ready for party?"

Zacharias smiled. "Martin, that is the problem with you camp dwellers. You are always in a rush! In good time. And yes, you will be invited."

They concentrated on the football match briefly. No one had scored yet. Martin dismissed it and turned to his Big friend. He was pleased with the guy. Someone fouled on the field.

"Stupid player. Even my little Matthew at home can play better than that."

"I know."

They watched the game some more and decided it was not worthy of their precious time.

"Staff club?"

Martin hesitated. He did not have the money to waste on beer anymore.

"I will pay," Zacharias added.

Martin accepted his generosity and followed Zacharias to his Honda that stood in a shade.

"I don't know if I already told you this, Martin, but did you know that John's daughter got the company scholarship?"

That was news to Martin who was already poised to mount the motorcycle. His left leg suspended in the air.

"She will be going to college?" Martin imagined her in one of those prestigious boarding secondary schools.

"Uh-huh. His children are really doing well. His first two boys are passing with flying colours in college and now his daughter will be the first girl ever in the history of the company to ever go to college. Imagine!"

"She passed? Are you sure about that, Zacharias? She passed and my brilliant son failed? My son, a boy failed and a stupid girl passed just like that? That is not possible!"

"Climb make we go."

Martin climbed onto the back of the motorcycle and they zoomed off.

"She passed with flying colours. This is true tok. It isn't cheating. Remember, she also passed common entrance in List A and first school Leaving with three credits."

"My goodness! My Peter passed in List B and failed the scholarship exam. My first boy wasn't even as good as John's third child." He reflected some more on the issue at hand.

"Zacharias, why is it that I have too much bad luck like this?"

"No, no, no! Not like that." He sped up enjoying the wind pounding hard on his happy face.

"Na true. See John; see you; see Isaac. Do you know that I am the only one who is still walking on foot?"

Zacharias did not respond.

"See Puis. He even owns a bicycle. Me, I cannot. Is it because I am dull or is it simply because God does not like me? He no like me at all! "

He sighed. "I should not have hopped on that truck like an animal that fateful morning to come to this god forsaken place, sef!"

"You don't know what you are talking about, Martin. See Puis. His daughter has two bastard children in the house and the girl is still just sixteen years. Plus, you know the kind of problem that I have? I don't think so and I won't tell you." He made a turn and stopped in the club's driveway.

"I am glad I came here. You know the kind of house I have in Bamenda? A big stone house for Foncha Street."

Martin's body went numb.

"You truly came here to kill me today, not so? Anyway, I will not die. Just take your bad luck and go away." He stepped off the motorcycle and headed home instead, deciding he was no longer interested in the free beer. Zacharias made no attempt to stop him.

Anastasia Tebi was so busy making market and feeding her family that she did not notice her husband return home. She had basins of stuff all over the parlour and kitchen for the children to sell and customers flowing in and out to purchase one item after another. Their house was a busy marketplace, Martin concluded and left her alone. He could feel a dull pain across his abdomen as he thought about what was going on in his home. The strangers, the smells, the food, the children, the wife, — busy, busy market place his home had become.

Dejected once more about the hand that fate had dealt him, he took to drinking palm wine and his favourite beer, Jobajo alone on the veranda. What was the use? Martin had asked himself this question a few more times before and each time he was at a loss of how best to respond. In his quiet corner of an already congested house he watched his children grow up. He watched the girls fail exam after exam as they spent their time helping Anastasia's trade. Then fortune smiled on his roof when Peter finally went to secondary school. He attended one far away in Bamenda where he lived with Anastasia's parents as he commuted to school daily. Martin was pleased. His wife had arrived at this decision without consulting with him. But he was pleased. Peter loved it there or so his letters communicated. That was all that mattered. He would be their own "somebody" in a world that judged families in terms of how many noteworthy or successful people came from a particular bloodline. If Martin was still not a Big Man, at least, Peter was on his way to becoming one, Martin rationalized. So Peter had cleaned his face with his little success washing away all the years of humiliation and embarrassment he had suffered. Martin could tell he was an emerging Big Man; first, the education, and next great things. It was such an easy formula for success and his son was on his way to mastering it. He felt so proud of his son, Peter, hoping that where he had failed, the boy would succeed in a big way and make them all really proud. Martin had never felt this happy, at least, not for a long, long time.

When he finished secondary school Peter aced the General Certificate of Education exams like it was nothing. People from all over the estate were pleasantly surprised wondering how Peter had managed to accomplish such a feat. There was so much buzz around this and Martin suspected he was back in the social business as a man who mattered. He was a proud Papa once more who had made the decision to dare into the wilderness to make this possible. Even John swallowed his pride and drove over to Martin's house to congratulate the "lad" on raising such a 'fine' son who was full of promise. "I knew your boy was a clever one," he said repeatedly looking around the tiny rooms that housed so many of Martin's off springs. Martin Tebi accepted his patronage and waited for John to say something else, but he didn't. However before leaving John gave the boy some money to celebrate his good fortune and advised him never to forget where he came from. Other well wishers stopped by and offered their own praises and gifts including Zacharias who was so stupefied by Peter's performance that he was short of words. Martin enjoyed that moment. Then he noticed Zacharias's wife sobbing on Anastasia's left shoulder and muttering that their children were all average at best failing one exam after another like poor people's children. Martin was surprised at this revelation. He watched

130

his friend cringe each time his wife spilled out more information about their family's ill fortunes.

"Is this true so, Zacharias?"

"Martin, like I told you, I have my own problems too," he said simply. When all the guests left Martin hugged his son and took him to Staff club for a befitting celebration only to find out that the place had changed significantly from what he was used to with different music, different styles and loud people with smelly armpits lounging around to watch a tennis match. But that day was his son's and nothing would ruin the experience for him.

When all the excitement had died down Peter began making arrangements for high school. His father watched him make clear plans on how to be a Big man in his own new world. It was the same thing only Peter was more methodical in his approach. Perhaps more like John. Martin smiled and hoped. He wished his son well and watched him leave home once more to seek his fortune elsewhere. John might have observed this too about Martin's son. He began spending his evenings with Martin again having empty conversations on topics they both seemed uninterested in. They would sit there and gaze into space for hours and occasionally share a bottle of beer and sighed many more times than they each realized. On one such evening he offered to take Martin over to his own club. Martin accepted and followed him there where he noticed a handful of people swimming in the pool, two European women included. They looked delicate in the pool in their skimpy swimming trunks. Martin looked away quickly muttering something.

"John?"

"It is none of your business." John shrugged his shoulders and explained that it was a white man thing.

"Alright."

Besides that the club was just as Martin had imagined it would be several times in his head as he spent those short two hours in the company of his Big friend. But the moment he returned home after the grand tour he fell into a deep depression. That could have been his life he mumbled to his wife all night long. He could have been part of that world had he stayed in the field. He could still hear the Black office supervisor drumming into his head that if he wanted to be a Big man, he should stick with the field. Those words rang in his head for the next couple of weeks. To make matters worse John would not leave him alone. He was there all the time now chatting about the days they all played draught together. Then one day he said they should start playing again. Martin concurred bringing out the old board game. The square boxes on the board had faded away gradually with the passage of time just like everything else was changing around them, including Martin and his four friends. The white squares blended with the black squares in a strange way so that each player now needed to lean backward to gauge where the boundaries ended and where the chip could possibly land. Martin and John would play the game not minding who took what colour or who was winning. They just played and kept playing not caring whether they enjoyed it or not and occasionally Lucy, Martin's daughter with Anastasia would bring them some refreshments, which most often was either water or a jug of palm wine Anastasia had secretly purchased for the two friends. When she appeared from the parlour with the refreshments in tow John's eyes would light up and he would praise the girl for being a gracious hostess even before she finished serving the drinks in the glasses that sat waiting on the veranda.

"Martin, your daughter is growing well these days."

"You think so?"

"But of course, my friend," he would pat him on the back and both would concentrate on the game.

This went on for a while until Martin unable to take it anymore, invited Puis to join them. Surprisingly, Puis accepted the invitation. After participating in a few of the sessions he became suspicious of John and told Martin to watch out. "Why the sudden interest in a game we all gave up a long time ago?"

Martin could not understand it too.

"Use a long spoon all the time when you eat with him, you hear?" Puis cautioned.

"Of course, I know that. You don't have to remind me. Is that not why I asked you to join us?"

Puis smiled. "You are my true friend, Martin; but I just thought I should warn you. These Big men like this, one never knows what they are up to!"

After a year John became Anastasia's good friend and she did not want to hear anything bad said about him. But one day the truth came out when Lucy announced that Mr. John had asked her to become his second wife. Martin was speechless. So it was Lucy all the time John was courting and not the game he was playing! When he regained his composure he drove the man away from his house and asked him never to step foot near their door again. Meanwhile he sent for his friend, Puis who came riding his bicycle as fast as he could.

"I knew it! The snake!"

"He is not a snake."

Martin and Puis looked at Anastasia.

"Your head no correct. So you agree say your child is fit to be but a second wife?"

She shook her head to the contrary and would say no more hoping that Martin and Puis would calm down. Instead they pressed on and finally she declared that she was not ready to discuss the details of the relationship with either one of them. When the gossip around the estate had subsided and John's wife had stopped badgering them with insults, Anastasia confronted her daughter about it. Lucy said she liked him and was ready to move into his house, if the parents gave their permission. Martin said "No," and Lucy threatened to have a child with him as his outside woman. Anastasia would not hear of this. She called Peter for more advice but he said it depended on whether his sister did not mind being married to an old man; if that were the case they should let her marry Mr. John. Martin would not listen and insisted that there would be no such union as long as he was alive. Confused, Ansastasia wrote to her favourite brother-in-law; Martin's brother came all the way from Nkwen to resolve the issue once and for all but Martin remained adamant. Lucy was his daughter and no one — friend or foe would steal her like that without proper courtship.

Everyone left him alone to continue to say "no" as he sulked day and night. For a while it worked until Martin spotted a young handsome ward servant flirting with Lucy. That did it. He would not tolerate Lucy having a relationship with a man whose future he could foretell was steeped in poverty. Not even if he were the poor man! What was a girl's chance with such a person? Misery all the way until one's death. No! Martin repeated in his head until he almost fell sick. Finally, he succumbed to John's wishes and without further ado he gave his blessings to the union between the Big man he was beginning to loathe even more and his beautiful daughter, and the ceremony was done in style in John's club. John had taken the trouble to invite only those who mattered and carefully left out the insignificant folks like Puis much to Martin's chagrin. But there wasn't much he could do to change John's mind. It was his day and it was his club and wedding. From then on Martin spotted Lucy being driven in a company car by a company driver to somewhere and from somewhere. Martin lips stretched out with a grin and he attempted a smile hoping that in letting John marry Lucy he had made the right decision for his daughter.

Chapter Twelve

With the departure of Peter and Lucy there was more room in the house for Martin and the rest of his brood. Sam, the one that came next failed the common entrance exams woefully but with Peter's help he managed to get into a commercial school. Attending the school thereafter was made possible with Lucy's new financial capability as the wife of a Big man. But Martin's children had to pay in kind and John made sure this happened holiday after holiday as he gave them holiday jobs in the fields, whether they sought one or not, to work with the labourers. And that was that! Martin though with misgivings, thanked his good stars and urged the sons to put their best foot forward for the entire estate to see. They were grateful in-laws and were determined to keep things that way not to embarrass their sister; neither did they want to lose their holiday jobs.

Meanwhile Anastasia was working harder to save whatever she could for her second daughter's education. Everyone had said their daughter Jennifer was the most brilliant girl around these days. The headmaster confirmed it and encouraged the Tebis to guide the girl properly. So Martin came up with a plan to tutor her at home. This strategy worked so well, for she did not only pass her exams but broke the divisional record in all subjects. She was unstoppable as she breezed through all the exams that had humiliated her older siblings before. Martin, who had expected Jennifer to perform well but not that well began puffing too. He might not be a Big man, he explained to John one evening, but he was certain his daughter would be Bigger than all four of them put together. John nodded. Martin was surprised.

"Did you just hear what I said?"

"I hear you alright. She is a clever *Girl*," John replied with an emphasis on the "Girl" part.

"So true. Clever girl like her father!"

Martin would wander into the bed bug club telling stories of how he used to lead his class in every subject. He sang his daughter's praises to John, Zacharias, Isaac, and Puis continuously explaining that she was a rare gem. He carried on in this manner until Puis laden with his own troubles told him off one day But Martin brushed him aside calling him a sour grape and boasted repeatedly that where he had failed, his daughter would pull him over the right way; not the Lucy way.

September came and Jennifer attended a prestigious government secondary school free of charge; books and all the necessary school supplies were part of the package. To top everything, she had also won the company scholarship and received an envelope stuffed with money to support her for the first year. They said it would be a violation for her to have both types of scholarship. Martin understood. They were jealous! At night, he confided in his wife that now that it was his family's turn to reap the benefits of their hard work everyone was jealous including the Big men who ran the company. Anastasia concurred and they both slept peacefully through the night.

As expected Jennifer 'crushed' her exams the first year around; however, in her second year she came running home with a note from the principal telling her parents not to bother sending her back to school. Martin asked her why, but Jennifer said it was just the way they did things at government schools. Martin had to concede that neither the principal's note nor Jennifer's response made any sense. When he shared his misgivings with his wife, she advised him to take it easy; so Martin relaxed. This brief moment of relaxation did not last long; instead it made him more restless. He needed to know the truth and no one was willing to tell him what this really was. Martin decided to see the headmaster about it; the respectable gentleman reassured him that it was nothing to worry about, especially since Jennifer was such a clever girl. Martin would like to believe this man who had been the first to see potential in her daughter, but there was something deep in his belly that doubted that all was fine. Having lost so many nights of precious sleep, he boarded a taxi one morning and went to Victoria to verify for himself. When he returned he took Jennifer into the bedroom and gave her the thrashing of her life; afterwards, he ordered her to stay indoors until he could figure out a solution or a way to further punish her. She did.

Week one came and passed with no sign of forgiveness on Martin's part. Week two was the same. As week three came around he began making arrangements to send her off to the village for a long break. This would have worked, if Chinedu and his wife had not started fighting over something. The weekend that Jennifer was supposed to disappear from the estate Chinedu's wife came crying with her six children tagging along. She needed a place to hide from her abusive husband, she told Martin. Someone had told her that Chinedu had been making plans to steal her children across the borders. No, no, no, Martin did not want that. Grinding his teeth he assured his daughter that it would not happen to his grandchildren. At this point he beckoned for Chinedu's wife and children to move into his already overcrowded home. He watched them squeeze in searching for room to place one item or their tired and hungry bodies. Once they all seemed to have settled down Martin rushed over to Chinedu's house and told him off. When he returned he had a bump on his forehead where he claimed he had hit his head in blind fury on a metal pole. Chinedu was not even at home, he claimed. How about that! Martin was so furious he called for his wife to quieten down Chinedu's

Vivian Sihshu Yenika

children. Anastasia just sighed and walked away shrugging
her shoulders all the way to her smoked filled kitchen. They
were not her problem. She could hear him in there grumbling
about something.

"As say-eh, Missus, am I not talking to you? Take those
bloody children them out of my sight. I have enough trouble
of my own to start worrying about another man's children."

Anastasia shouted back from the kitchen suggesting that
he should ask but his daughter who was the real owner of
the children to do something about it. He ignored the
suggestion and focused on his wife. "But I am asking you.
It is you who is my wife. Do something about this!" He
sounded a little irritated.

"Okay." She came out of the kitchen all covered in soot
and grabbed the children by the wrists mumbling on her
way out to search for their mother.

"I can hear you."

She slammed the front door behind her once they were
on the veranda.

"There, go join your Mami," she said releasing them.
Chinedu's wife sat there oblivious to what was happening.
Her eyes faltered shifting from one child to the other
watching them dash into the yard and began rolling on the
ground playing a game she did not understand. Anastasia
also observed the children making merry. Her eyes lit up
and she adjusted her wrapper around her waist before
heading back to the kitchen. There was peace once more in
the house. However this was short-lived.

Jennifer was on her way to join the children out playing
in the yard when Martin bumped into her by the door that
led to the sole bedroom. "You again? You so, what will I do
with you? Eh? Get out of my sight you good for nothing
girl. One sends you to school and you go and begin to make
foolish."

The girl brushed past him to leave the room but he extended one hand and dragged her by the ear, pulling her in different directions.

"Come back here and tell me about the bastard who put you in the family way, you stupid thing with your face like an 'ashawo'."

"Papa, I don't know."

This irritated him even more. "You don't know-eh?" He slapped her and double backhanded her again and again. Jennifer began to sob.

"Cry your crocodile tears, foolish thing. 'I don't know.' When will you ever know something? How many men does it take to father a child?"

Martin entered the bedroom and slumped on the bed rambling on and on about the disgrace that Jennifer had brought upon their family. He was still raging on about this without a care while his clever daughter sobbed out her humiliation in the parlour. The sound of her sobs irked him so much, he burst out of the room and once again pulled her ear dragging her back into the bedroom. "And one thing, if you tell anybody you are with child, you are dead. Do you hear me?"

She nodded.

"Get out of here." He stared at her pitiful face and his heart softened.

"Just go with your bad luck." He closed his eyes to repress the image of his pregnant clever daughter and pretended that it was not happening to his family. With his eyes still shut, he paced the overcrowded bedroom walking back and forth and kicking everything in his path. Finally, he returned to the parlour and buried his head in his lap for a while.

"Where's that Chinedu's wife, sef?" He yelled at no one in particular.

"Anastasia, where is she?"

"Papa Peter, she is outside."

"Where?"

Chinedu's wife entered the parlour.

"You want to see me?"

"Take this money and leave my family alone. Go anywhere. Go find your Mama or your grandmamma in the village. I have my own troubles too. Oya, take your battalion them go hide elsewhere." He dismissed her out of his sight but she remained standing there.

"You are going, not so?"

She looked away and started fidgeting with the edge of her loincloth it twirling her finger.

"You are going right this instant!" It was an order this time.

Chinedu's wife stopped twirling the end of her loincloth and gazed at the pathetic man who was telling her what to do, and walked away. "I am going nowhere."

"What did you say?" Martin screamed after her.

"I say, I am going nowhere!" She screamed back and slammed the front door behind him.

"Weh! A house packed with bad luck children." Martin let his deflated body drop into his favourite sofa and buttocks almost touched the floor. He felt old and helpless. Why all these troubles on this one person? he thought.

Later that evening when Chinedu came to reclaim his family, Martin was also waiting for him. After giving him his piece of mind, he demanded that Chinedu promise never to steal his children across the border. The younger man promised and Martin was relieved. He was so content that he forgot about Jennifer's problems for that moment assuring himself that they could a few more days.

But during the week Chinedu's wife kept coming over to visit her father twice daily. Martin could not understand why and did not believe it was from genuine love for him as a father. He just watched her climb on the veranda, take Jennifer for a stroll and enter into the kitchen to eat whatever was available and eventually left without a word to Martin. He admitted the child was trouble and would always remain trouble so he left her alone and concentrated on his own life. However, it was not too long after these frequent visits from his oldest daughter that Martin found Jennifer wriggling in pain one evening on the floor. She complained of deadly cramps squeezing her abdomen to subdue the pain, and rolling on the floor. Moments later Martin noticed blood on the floor where she lay wriggling in pain. Tears flooded his eyes and he dropped onto his knees and hugged his daughter. He could see more blood on the floor. Martin began weeping for her.

"Where is it hurting, my daughter?" He tried to get her to explain but she was in too much pain and Anastasia was somewhere selling something.

"Where again?" Martin bundled his clever daughter and rushed her to the hospital. It was an emergency and the hospital was in commotion. When it was over the hospital staffs let Jennifer -rest and advised Martin to take a nap himself on the vacant bed right next to his daughter there in the female ward. Martin thanked his colleagues. He felt sorry for himself, for his children, and for his wife. What kind of parent was he? And why was Anastasia not looking for a better man to take better care of her? He pondered over all these questions praying that nothing bad should happen to the only child that he had with more potential than the hundreds running around everywhere.

After Jennifer recovered she explained to the nurses and her parents that her half-sister had been treating her condition with a bluish substance and when it was not working as fast as they had anticipated she had decided to take an over dose of nivaquine.

"And a clever girl like you could not figure out that that would be bad?" He sighed. "Look at who I am talking to." Martin balled his fist to punch her face but quickly changed his mind as he noticed eyebrows rousing and heads already shaking in disapproval. He dared not box her face as he would have liked to at that moment; at least, not in the hospital. What would his colleagues think of him?

The nurse-in-charge warned Jennifer and insisted that she never take chances again with her young life, for she might not be as lucky next time. When they discharged Jennifer, Martin took her home and immediately sent word to Chinedu banning his wife from ever setting her feet into his home again. Hours later, Chinedu came running to plead on her behalf, but Martin said she was a badly brought up girl bent on ruining his life. Chinedu understood why Martin felt that way but insisted that his wife could change. Martin scoffed at the idea of her changing and simply reiterated his point of not wanting her in their home.

On leaving his father-in-law's house, Chinedu returned home and sparing no detail explained what had happened. He advised her to leave her father and his family alone, so they could all live in peace. Instead, she cursed them both and replied that she would do what was right for her, At that moment the right thing as she explained to Chinedu was to spend more time with Jennifer whether the two men liked it or not. No one was going to tell her how to live her life, she explained further to her husband; and the very evening they had this conversation Chinedu's wife visited the Tebis. Martin, getting more upset on seeing her at his doorstep slammed the door in her face, but she stood there and waited knocking intermittently.

"Just go back where you came from," Martin shouted from inside.

"And where be that?" She knocked harder but no one came to open the door for her. She went to the back door and knocked again hoping that her stepmother would respond. But no one did. She sighed.

"Okay, ah go come back." No one was going to keep her out of that house. When Chinedu heard about this he was dismayed and asked her why she liked to embarrass him like that. She ignored him. Chinedu had had it with a woman who listened to nobody, not to her father, not to her husband and not even to her rational self. One morning when she left the house without bothering to inform Chinedu again, he seized the opportunity and acted as he felt he should have done a long while ago; he gathered his children, packed a few items here and there and took along with him to a secret beach to flee the country. He was about to board an engine boat with all of them when one of his fellow travellers commented that the first child did not resemble him at all. He took one look at the child's face and concurred. Immediately, he gave the child some money for taxi and left him to find his way back to his mother. The engine boat sped away with the rest of the family.

When Magda's daughter saw a customs officer holding her first child in front of the company's main office she broke down and cried like she had not done since she was born. She wailed and wailed cursing the day she was born to irresponsible parents and the day she was forced to marry an irresponsible stranger who had stolen all her kids and was now rejecting her favourite child of all. People sympathized with her at first but when they heard where she had been and why she had gone there, they lost their patience and dismissed her as the irresponsible one. Magda's child told them off and moved back into Martin's house. It was like a sequel to a nightmare Martin had already had lived through and barely survived to tell the story; only this time it seemed much more real and extremely difficult to wish it away.

Martin left her alone to do what she wanted. And she whined, pined and accused everyone of some kind of wrongdoing. They tried to ignore her in vain. From morning to night she would sit on the veranda crying and explaining to anybody who would listen that Martin was not paying attention to her because she was an "outside child". She threatened to go and report him to the welfare people but thought twice about this and decided against it. She would wail that she was an orphan who had been abandoned by the world just because "her own no dey!" – She was a nobody whom no one cared a thing about her, not even her parents, she sang as she wept. Martin's neighbours tired of the daily drama they were fast becoming a part of, summoned him. He was to resolve the issue or pay weekly fines for disturbing the peace of the neighbourhood. They threatened that if it did not act accordingly, they would take up the matter with the company officials. Martin thought about the situation night after night and decided to consult with Isaac on the problem. Isaac told Martin his daughter could start working immediately in the palm kernel room, if she was interested. When Martin discussed the terms of the employment with his daughter she actually agreed to give the job a shot, and left them in peace moving into her own house far away from the Tebis.

With Chinedu's wife taken care of Martin could now direct his undivided attention to Jennifer who looked meeker than ever helping around the house with the chores. She still refused to tell them who had impregnated her. They let her alone until one find day she decided to speak; it was the vice principal of their school. On hearing this news Martin boarded a taxi and went back to Victoria to plead his daughter's case. The Principal said he could not change his recommendations just because he came pleading, for if he let Jennifer back in, he would be condoning a lifestyle the school was vehemently opposed to. The girl must be punished for bad behaviour, he insisted in a stern voice. Martin was shocked, embarrassed, and disappointed all at once. He could not believe that even Bigger Men, more so,

144

those employed by the government could be this petty. Or worse yet, that they could be so outright cold-hearted. He weighed his options carefully in his mind as the little man whom he was, now standing in the presence of one of the most powerful and highly respected principals in the country – or so people had confided. Perhaps he should go home and make other arrangements for his daughter, he contemplated overwhelmed with the weight of the defeat he had just experienced. The furrows on his forehead deepened as he struggled to find a workable solution in his mind. Bad idea to have come, he concluded. The more he thought about it, the more he realized all the forces at play. He was a small man, he conceded; but who would not do the same, if they were in his shoes? However, when he also remembered that his Jennifer was one of the most brilliant students in her class as was indicated in her report card, and deserved to be in a top school like that he mustered more courage and approached the Principal again.

"Please, sir, I beg of you to consider re-admitting my Jennifer." His voice faltered as he anticipated the man's response.

"I thought I made myself clear to you already?"

Martin laughed hysterically. "I know, sir; but I just thought you will forgive her since she has so much sense in her head. She is my only eye, sir."

The Principal ignored him and continued fidgeting with something. Martin waited patiently. Time was all he had. There was no need to rush. After waiting for a while he explained further that since no one knew about the dismissal and the pregnancy – especially now that Jennifer was back to normal due to an unfortunate miscarriage it would be okay to re-admit her. The principal eyed Martin with so much disdain that Martin wished he was back home. In spite of this he stood there and waited.

"So she is no longer with child, you say?"

"Yes, sir." Martin replied, watching the Big man with a little trepidation as the Principal adjusted his buttocks in his comfortable chair not caring whether Martin's legs were tired of carrying his plump body or not.

"I was right about your daughter after all. She is not a good example for our students." He stood up. "Mr. Tebi, there is nothing more I can do for you. She is a rotten cocoyam and must stay far away from here." He began tidying up his desk. Martin waited for him to say something more. The principal looked at the pathetic father standing there in a white cotton shirt that was now drenched with sweat, waiting for him to perform magic so his daughter would automatically become a good girl, and became distracted.

"You need anything else?"

"Yes, sir. I beg of you to consider re-admitting her. My daughter like this is the only one with sense in my whole family. I need help; please sir."

He dropped onto his knees and begged the Big man who grew stiff and pretended not to notice that the father of one of his students was hanging on to his trousers and almost in tears.

"Is that all?" He said looking away.

Martin was disheartened as he stood up and wiped off sweat from his face on his shirt sleeve.

"Okay. Is that how things will be, sir?"

The Principal waited for him to leave. Martin headed for the door and that was when he noticed the vice principal out in the corridor chatting with someone whom Martin deemed very important from the nice suit he had on. There was no time to wait. Martin dashed forward grabbed the vice principal by the tie and dragged him along with him back to the Principal's office. "Now, Mr. Principal do something. This is the father of Jennifer's miscarried child. Will you do something or you want me to take it to the newspaper. I can even broadcastam on radio Buea? Which is which?"

The vice principal looked confused. "Sir, what is this all about?" He managed to ask as he struggled to pull his neck out of Martin's clutch.

The Principal looked away.

"Eh? Or do you want me to take it to the SDO?"

The principal's expression changed. "Nothing like that, Mr. Tebi. Come in and take a seat. No need for that now." He beckoned for him to come back into the office. Martin Tebi dragged the vice principal along; this time by the arm and they shut the door after them.

"Okay. She will stay with us."

Martin let go the vice principal. "Thank you, sir. Thank you plenty. I will tell my Jennifer let her stay far away from this bad man; I swear to God, sir. It will not happen again, sir."

The principal barely looked at the vice principal's direction.

They shook hands and Martin left the two Big Men in peace to sort out whatever it was they needed to sort out as Big Men heading such a prestigious school. He too would go search for his own peace in his small home.

As his taxi entered the confines of the estate he could see the smoke in the air merging with some clouds. All white and sometimes gray far, far above everything. He could also smell the rich aroma of the cooked palm fruits as he listened carefully for the factory clock to chime the time. He breathed hard and sighed long sniffing the air one more time before the bus ground to a halt at the makeshift park. He was back home where he belonged.

Chapter Thirteen

All was quiet on the estate as people performed their routine tasks. The people in the office filled their ledgers and typed something or did something that Martin never understood and did not care to understand. The people in the hospital healed and healed patients, who came out of there smelling like medicine and bursting with renewed energy; the people out there in the fields... Hmmm! Martin reflected on that aspect of the company experience for a much longer time than he would have liked as he wondered why many of those headmen and field overseers got rewarded more often than everyone else. What made them so special on the plantation?. They worked, those people out there in the fields, those harvesters but it was the people who ran around the field all day with big ledgers clasped tightly under their armpits and every once in a while brought them out from there to check off names that got promoted! He had been one of those ledger carriers, an up and coming Big man, he remembered vaguely; but he had also been a big coward or so he would like to explain to any who cared to ask or listen. Fortunately, no one was that interested in his pathetic life.

Martin Tebi was put on the two to nine shift. He liked this shift better than the morning shift since he did not have to deal with too many Big people. As a matter of fact, he had to deal with only two: the nurse-in-charge and the doctor who popped in once to make one final round before leaving him alone to sit in his own office in the male ward and watch over the sick who saw him as god in his own right. The hours would tick slowly by as he read old copies of the *Nursing Mirror*, learning new medical jargon here and there like his medical colleagues. But once it was time, he would wash his hands in some kind of solution and carefully adjust his overalls before flickering the lights to warn the replacement staff of his departure. Martin had grown to love this shift. It was peaceful and gave him ample time to reflect as he advanced in years wondering daily how that had happened. There were times he would sit there lost in thoughts with the *Nursing Mirror* opened in front of him. Had it been worth it leaving all with which he was familiar up north to come try his luck in the coast? He did not know for sure anymore. But Puis had shown him a picture of his relatives in the village and they looked like beggars. Perhaps he would have ended up like one of those people in the picture. He shook his head to the contrary as he left for the night. He was an educated man poised to take over from the Europeans; he could never have ended up like them. If not with this company, perhaps it would have been something with the government like some of his friends who had not bothered to jump into the truck that fateful day. These thoughts crept on his mind sometimes making him sad. But why?

At last, he would leave for home whistling as he paused every now and then to appreciate the bright stars above him. He did not understand why he was strangely drawn to these stars so much. He would pause on his tracks and attempt to count them one at a time only to drop the counting mid way and let his eyes feast on the dazzling natural lights. They shone far above him providing him with just enough light to find his way home to keep his family company. He was grateful for that believing that sometimes they worked better than the company flashlights he carried on him during night duty shifts. Where the flashlight concentrated on single spots, the stars brightened everywhere and equally generously sharing its natural light for all to take advantage of. It was all intensely dark or all fairly bright. No cheating!

Martin began playing draught more often now with Puis as they reflected on the choices they had made almost thirty years ago. The two friends would sit there lost in the game while the night wore off as though nothing else mattered. Did anything else matter anymore, Martin wondered. They played not caring who won or lost. They simply played to fill the void in their lives. And every so often a child would extend greetings and they would respond in a sing-song manner, or a nosy neighbour would stop by to see what they were *really* doing. At times, these would be younger single females there to comment on how large Mr. Martin's stomach had grown larger over the years. He would tell them off and concentrate on the game not letting them see the sadness that was buried deep in his eyes; or notice the creases on his forehead that multiplied. But they did anyway and would stroll away whispering something he could never hear.

Before going to bed he would stare at his pot belly and touch the ridges that had formed on the sides of his waist and wonder where he had been all these while when these were happening. His wife told him that he had been busy playing life. He told her off and looked at her own body that still looked – well – he did not know how to describe it. Some parts looked good and others looked terrible. How could a young woman have aged so fast? Then he remembered that she was married to a nobody, and had to trade like a common woman to supplement his income. Well, she was his woman! Who would touch a second hand cargo, especially one with too many mouths to feed like Anastasia? He felt completely safe in that domain. He reflected some more, thinking about the amount of energy she still had. Was he really safe? He was not too sure anymore. These days he was not sure about many things. Anastasia was the one thing he was certain about – the loyal wife to a small man; worse yet, a man who could not even take care of his own family and had to beg his wife to help. Weh! He

151

exclaimed in his mind and as always in pidgin English and never in his mother tongue whatever that was anymore. He reflected some more and concluded that she was not like Magda's daughter who went looking for people to take care of her but had become an independent work horse with enough energy to spare. Thinking of Magda's daughter, Chinedu's wife, Martin laughed. That one was too much he had long concluded, and from what he heard another foolish man had opted to take her in. Wonders would never end! Martin cupped his chin as he thought about this daughter of his. He had to admit that she was something though. He did not know anymore. He was just happy she was out of his life, just as he was thankful that Anastasia still had the energy to help him keep the family afloat.

Years ago he had come to the company firm and trim but now he looked like an inflated balloon that just floated. He thought about this; thought about his progressively gray hairline and how hard his wife tried night after night to ward the grayness off with Morgan's pomade, and concluded that life was not fair. He would look at the remains of his once beautiful furniture and wonder why his wife had not bothered to make his living room a little more appealing like those he saw in "loose" women's homes. He was always thinking about one thing or the other. Indeed, fate had not been kind to him, he concluded again one night when he returned and found two huge men waiting for him in his parlour. He did not know who they were and did not bother to find out although this did not stop them from volunteering the information. They were his sons by Joanna and Magda from long ago! What was this too na? He wondered out loud asking under his breath why God would not leave him to rest even for one moment. No such luck. One of the boys said he needed money for capital to start his own business; the other said he needed a job right away. When he asked them why they thought he could help them out, one replied that his mother had mentioned something about him being a Big man with the company; meanwhile the other simply grinned and nodded in agreement. Martin smiled. Perhaps he was a Big man after all. Nevertheless, when they went out he asked his wife to bolt the door twice and not let anyone in until he was ready. She did just that, but he still could not sleep well. Early in the morning he sent for Chinedu's wife explaining the situation but she sent word back that she wanted no part of the family reunion. They were not her responsibility and that was that. Martin humbled himself and went over to see her in her house for the first time since she started working. Despite this grand gesture on his part she still refused to be part of it.

Martin did not know what else to do. The huge men were in his parlour every morning and would not leave until late at night when they had finished off all the food meant for the smaller children who really needed it. He never asked them where they lived and they did not volunteer the information. Not long afterwards money started disappearing in the house. First, it was little change here and there; later it became huge sums of money. That was when Anastasia got angry and packed her things to leave unless Martin dealt with the situation at hand. She explained to him that she could handle any kind of disruption to her family life but she drew the line when people started messing with her market money. Martin begged her not to leave him alone with strangers who could be murderers. She took one look at him and told him to go kill himself, for he was not worthy of any sympathy.

"Eh, Anastasia? You want me to do what?"

She was already dragging a suitcase from under the bed and a bundle of her other stuff carefully wrapped in an old loincloth.

"You heard me."

153

He was tired of her rubbish. "What kind of mother are you that would run away from children?"

She gave him a funny look.

"Okay, I understand, Mama; but please, don't leave me alone with thieves. They will kill me and take my bank book and then what will you tell my relatives?"

"Please, sah, I am not the thief man," one of the son's pleaded.

"Shut up, you idiot! Some man ask you?" Martin turned to his wife for understanding and a little bit of kindness.

"Papa Peter, leave me let me go."

"Ah, ah, Anastasia, how can you just go like that after all these years

"Watch me." She searched the room with her eyes. "You see my credit union book?"

Martin looked surprised. He did not even know she had a book like that. Anastasia started crying believing they had finally stolen her book. Now Martin was truly mad. He burst into the parlour where the two huge men sat munching something without a care in the world.

"Which of you two be the thief man, again? Answer me!"

Joanna's son pointed at his cousin. Martin walked over to where the man sat. "You? You came to my house and made my Missus cry? You think say she strong like your bad mama? Get out of my house.

The younger man stared at him in the eye and walked away.

"Now we truly know who did it." Martin felt relieved. "I always knew that Joanna was a good girl." He scratched his head and looked at his son. "Where is your mother now?"

The huge man sighed. "No be ah say she don marry and the Oga no want see me with eye sef?"

Martin scratched his head again and looked away. "I see." He could empathize with Joanna's husband as he wondered who really wanted a glutton for a son. Anastasia stood by the door waiting for him to say something else. He shooed her away and she caved in taking her suitcase back into the bedroom and began rearranging her stuff. She was back in his life.

"What is your name, son?"

"Jacob, sah."

He frowned at the name as he thought some more scratching his head. "Not to worry, we will find you work. You be good boy." From the corner of his eyes he stole glances at Jacob standing tall there and looking trim and fit. He reminded him of himself when he was that age. Only the child looked pathetic in trousers that hung around his waist by the generosity of a cover crop string. Had he looked equally ramshackle when he had first arrived? Martin took pity on him and humbled himself once more to seek assistance from a real Big man. Jacob got a job in the fields.

He lived with the Tebis for sometime before moving into his own place to start life as the professional labourer he was fast becoming. Meanwhile Magda's children were creating scandal after scandal as they fought in Chinedu's wife's house where the thief brother had found his way to. One day, he beat her up so badly that she was hospitalized. Martin cried when he saw how badly damaged his beautiful daughter's face had become. Why on earth would someone beat his own sister like that na? He wondered about this crying his eyes out at night and spending most of his spare time in the hospital nursing the woman back to health. When she was stronger he confronted her brother about the incident and he simply said he had seen her in a white man's car.

"What?"

A white man who drove a white Mazda, he explained. Martin could not believe such an allegation.

"Why do you hate your sister so much na, son?"

He shook his head to the contrary. Martin asked Chinedu's wife about it and she told him to get out of her sight. Martin left her alone and returned to his friends for company. A week after Chinedu's wife was discharged from the hospital her brother got a job somewhere. She was so grateful that she prepared a special meal and brought it over to her father's house to thank him. Martin was equally touched by this gesture; he hugged her long and thanked her for having a heart in that her thick chest after all.

But his happiness did not last long as Martin also began spotting Chinedu's wife in that white man's car in broad daylight. After work, the two would drive away somewhere just like his son had described. Puis had also seen them kissing in the nursery where she worked picking kernels. He said he wanted it stopped immediately or else he would sever all ties with the Tebis. Martin begged his daughter to put a stop to this foolishness, but she told him repeatedly that she was enjoying her life and that Martin should stay out of her business. Martin got out of her sight and left her alone. After all, he too had shame. Puis decided to take matters into his hands. He pooped in the man's car twice as he visited the "loose woman." The man wised up and started packing his car up on a hill a little further from the residential quarters where he visited Chinedu's wife. Puis did not give up either, for no white man was going to bring so much shame to his friend's family. He would wait until the headlights were out and then watch how Mr. F. as he referred to him, descended the small elevation hastily to see "his woman." Once out of the way, Puis would then slash a tire and leave a note warning Mr. F. to stay off their camp. The man did not care. He stayed by "his woman" and visited her in her one-room house right there in the heart of the camp for all to see. This burned Martin's stomach and he banished Chinedu's wife from his life forever, or so he told his wife. And she nodded.

Puis tried every trick he had once used on people he did not like but none worked on this man. Then he learned at work that the man was not a true white man. Martin was glad with this news. But he looked white. Martin was confused. Puis explained that where he came from some of them looked like that. The news spread with Chinedu's wife being the news spreader herself showing pictures of the man in his home country bossing other white "cutting mbangas" just like the harvesters who had forced Martin out of the fields. It all began to make sense to Puis who had also spent sleepless nights second guessing himself as to why his scare tactics were not working on the man. And one evening he told Martin that Mr. F. was the strongest white man he had ever seen in his entire life but never bothered to explain any further; and Martin never bothered to find out why he said so.

Their friend Zacharias was finally made a manager and he threw a party of parties to show how worthy he was of the post. At the party he enjoyed himself so much that he forgot that he was just a man like Martin and the others, and got stupidly drunk. On his way home to join his wife and children he ran under a company truck that was packed by the road and died like a fowl. Martin wept for his friend asking why God could be so cruel at times. But Puis retorted that at least, he had died a Big man. It was fate.

"How can a man just go and kill himself like that?"

"No, he did not kill himself, Martin. It was an accident. And he had a satisfied grin on his face; did you not see it?"

Martin chuckled then wiped off a tear from his eye. "Difference dey? He drank and he died. How does this differ from him killing himself?"

"Boh, you surprise me sometimes. It is really simple. Money killed him." Puis was adamant about this. He did not want to waste his time on things that could be explained easily like Zacharias' death. Martin was shocked. "For where? Not money; too much glad that he will have too much money killed him. Anticipation of wealth can really be bad!"

"That, I agree with. You are so right; too much glad about money can be dangerous." Now that they were on the same page they decided to leave the mortuary where Zacharias' corpse lay. "Did you hear what the woman was saying out there?"

"Martin, you listen too much. My friend is dead and that is what concerns me now.

Martin chuckled again, "She said, who go take care of 'my battalion' now-oh! Stupid woman! A man dies and she is concerned only about who will take care of her and the children!"

Puis started laughing. "And your own there is what?"

"I'm serious. That was what she was saying. Stupid woman."

Puis sighed and walked further away from the crowd that stood waiting for the company officials to do something.

"He died like a fowl, Boh. They say his neck got twisted and he bled to death with no one there to help him, even the witch doctor who made his promotion possible!"

Martin shrugged this away and gave his friend a funny look.

From then on Martin decided to stop worrying about the fact that he was not a real Big man. He also stopped worrying about his children and their never-ending problems. He was just grateful that he was still alive. He had seen the company truck conveying Zacharias' corpse, family and property back to his place of origin. He had seen Zacharias' job being given to a man who had just graduated from the university, a man younger than Magda's son. He had seen the boy proudly moving into the house that would have been Zacharias' and the boy was driving around chasing young girls just like Zacharias would have done. Nothing made sense anymore and it pained him that a young man with little or no experience could take over and just live the life others had put in all they had to build the company.

"Anastasia, how can a man work so hard and die while a small catarrh nose boy fresh from school got it all without shedding a drop of sweat? Eh?"

"Papa Peter, leave me let me sleep," Anastasia answered back adjusting her blanket.

"Truly, how sad is that, eh Anastasia?" He turned around to face her on the bed but she was already snoring.

Once more, Martin withdrew from society. The only social functions he attended were funerals and church celebrations. And he would sit in an inconspicuous corner and watch what was happening right in front of him. He loved that.

There were days that he found himself strolling among the palm trees enjoying the peace that reigned there as he thought of nothing.

The aroma of freshly cooked palm fruits would hit his nose and he would smile and wait for the factory clock to chime the time alerting him of his responsibilities that lie somewhere in the hospital and in the camps. The palm fronds muffled and he watched them settle taking their respective places on the different branches. As he strolled in the evenings through this quiet bush of palm trees he understood why the early Europeans enjoyed strolling there often. Hoisting himself up a piece of jagged rock that lay carelessly on the fertile land was difficult and Martin would smile and tell himself that he was getting old. In a few years he would be ready to go back where he had come from. The thought of this made him sad as he had grown to love this place so much that he would really like to die there. But that would not be proper. His parents had died and his older brother who was now the head of the family had said there was room in the family house in the village for all of them.

Martin knew he would have to return home sometime, but for now he did not want to think about it. Not far away from where he sat, he saw a snake drop off a palm tree and slither away. He was feeling too lethargic to run away from this deadly reptile. So he pretended he hadn't seen it and let it slide far away from him to some other place where he was certain it would bite some unfortunate labourer or would eventually get killed by a fortunate hunter. He could hear the factory purring and spewing more smoke, and the boilers grinding loud and humming as they toiled on to serve every one. The factory was getting old too, just like him. Martin sighed.

Chapter Fourteen

When he returned home from his walk in the palm bush he was greeted by the cheerful voices of young kids as they ran around all over the place playing without a care. Seeing them like that brought back memories of his children. Was Peter still the happy person who had left them awhile ago in pursuit of bigger dreams? Was he happy out there in Douala? He wished he knew. He had heard lots of bad things about the congested city and had never had the courage to go find out for himself. They said food was dear; houses were dear, and thieves were not only trained but armed with weapons. How could one live in a place like that? But Peter had assured him in a letter that he loved his life and the noise that surrounded his home and that was that. Martin doubted that anybody could love such a life. His other son, Sam was a clerk on a rubber plantation in Victoria. Martin knew that it was a dead end job and that his son would retire a clerk, even though his son was not yet aware of this. If only he could convince him about this perhaps he could help him become a Big man someday. But how did one tell a child that his life was already a dead end before he even started it. If only he was brave enough to do just that, perhaps things would be different. But he had never really considered himself a brave man in that sense. His daughters, well, they would have no problem as long as they married well. A thought crossed his mind and he laughed softly. Jennifer would marry the man and not the man marrying her. He hoped he would live to see this happen with his daughter being the Big "man" and her husband just following her along waiting for her to throw some change his way. That would be something to see. But

161

just what if she erred in judgment again? Martin shook his head and climbed onto the veranda to wait for his wife.

As he sat there he saw his children's future flashing through, with Chinedu's wife crying because the imitation Whiteman had finally returned home without taking her along. Wasn't she his sweet heart? Martin said she was, and sent the thought flying in the direction where it had come. He smiled. He would like to think that they would all do fine. What else was left for him to do?

The draught board lay shattered under his bed with Anastasia's market stuff on top of the pieces. He could not begin to fathom where any of the game pieces were anymore and his friends did not come over as often again. Puis, sometimes, but the others were busy being imitation white men in their big houses in the residential quarters once meant only for the Europeans. It could have been his life if he had only listened and taken all the abuse out there. But no, he was not strong enough to handle the challenges that came with the job; hence had to deprive himself of the perks as well. He had made that choice a long time ago not knowing what lay down the road for him and his family.

These days he sat on the veranda whenever he was not at work watching the tractors and trucks drive by, women gossiping, and children playing. Everyone had begun referring to him as Papa and he knew what that meant. It was just a matter of time. A couple more years at the most before it would be his turn to pack up and make way for a new recruit with that special dream of becoming Big and talents to pawn to the company. He had been in this mood for some months when Isaac stopped by to find out the whereabouts of Chinedu's wife. Martin did not know where she was and he told his friend so.

"That makes it easier for me then," Isaac replied.

"How so?" Martin was unsure. He was also tired of explaining his children's actions to people. "She has absconded!" Isaac laughed, "That will be the official report instead of me sacking the stupid girl who thought that because she was hanging out with the manager she was important."

"Absconded or sacked, what do I care? Is it not her life?" Martin dismissed the threat.

He never heard anymore news about Chinedu's wife until someone said he saw her taking a boat to cross over to join her husband. Martin clapped his hands in wonder. He did not know whether to rejoice or to feel sad. He felt numb but gradually his face began to fluster. Let her go wherever it pleases her, he mumbled to himself and decided not to dwell on the news any further.

All was going well with Martin until he accidentally stepped on a rusty nail one night on his way to the public latrine. Martin pulled it out and began treating himself at home. He treated himself every day limping to work without letting anyone know he was hurt. Instead of his foot getting better it began to smell. His wife drew his attention to this one night as she was massaging it with some hot water. Martin dismissed her concerns and poured more ointment into the hole that the nail had so carefully bored deep under his sole. He continued to hide his condition from his colleagues and struggled to heal himself at home. When they asked why he was limping, he always replied nothing was the matter. It went on like that until he started running a temperature. The nurse in charge asked him why he had a soiled bandage around his feet and he said it was nothing. The nurse drew the superintendent's attention to this and he asked Martin what had happened. Martin said it was nothing to worry about.

"Is that so?"

Martin nodded.

"Okay, Martin, if a patient comes with a similar complaint what will you, as a medical person do?

"I'll treat him and give him anti-tetanus injection, sir."

"Have you given yourself the shot?"

Martin processed the question in his mind much longer than would have been expected.

"Martin?"

"No, sir." Martin replied sheepishly. He saw where the interrogation was going.

The superintendent looked concerned.

"And how many days again since you stepped on a nail?"

Martin counted in his head and the blood drained from his face.

"I see, Martin." His Black boss started to leave then he turned back. "What is really wrong with your head, Martin? You have worked with six European doctors and you still don't know A from B?"

Martin remained quiet, balls of sweat were already gathering around his forehead. The Black boss sighed.

"It is time to do something. Get ready at once!"

"Yes, sir."

The superintendent alerted all the nurses on duty and medical charts were filled out, a bed was made and in no time Martin was their patient.

He sent word to Anastasia that he had arranged for Martin to be admitted at once.

The next days and weeks there was a lot of commotion around the hospital as everyone fussed over Martin. They checked this, gave him that, changed that just to keep him alive. His temperature went up then down. Nurse Paddy checked his pulse one morning and could not find one. He panicked. "Doctor, doctor come-oh. Temperature is up, up and up. Mr. Paul, help me. Somebody help me here-oh let this man not die in my hands." He was babbling as he feared the worse for their well-respected colleague. Soon the hospital was crowded. Martin who had succumbed into a nice slumber heard someone crying. He opened his eyes and saw his wife standing by his bedside. There were too many people around. He wondered what they were all doing in his room. He noticed some peeking through the window. Wait a minute. Where was he? He looked around and realized that he was in a special room. Someone had transferred him to the room reserved for management. He could recognize the doctor's face. The medical superintendent whispered something to a group of real nurses who were attending to him. Then Martin spotted some of the managers outside the door. Everyone was there including the Black manager who had advised him some several years ago to choose the fields instead of office work. Martin felt important and attempted a faint smile. His wife held on to his hand and began whimpering as Martin's eyelids fluttered. One last smile and a final breath. The factory blasted the time. It was four p.m. on the dot and the pungent aroma of the cooked palm fruits filled the room almost choking everyone in there, including Martin as he inhaled one last time and never exhaled. Martin was dead just like that.

Mrs. Tebi began rolling on the floor as the doctor confirmed her husband's death.

"Martin-oh, Martin-oh, Wetin ah go do without you-oh?" she wailed rolling from one end of the room to the other. Puis grabbed her by the wrist and dragged her away from the dead body. He too was crying but in a manly way squeezing his eye lids tight until his eyes became red and then facing the other way for the tears to dry up.

"Mr. Puis, na your friend that, cold like ice. He di sleep like firewood. Eh, Mr. Puis?"

"Missus, I understand. Just tie heart. Na God's work. He is not a log of wood; just in a deep slumber as the Lord had planned it all along."

"God's work how? Na witch." She was now rolling on the ground outside the hospital doubting if her husband's death was an act of God or as a result of witchcraft.

"My Jennifer, Martin's eye, what will I tell her? Say your Papa no wait to see your degree. Eh, Mr. Puis? Did we not pray enough? Did we not pass confession? Did we not work hard enough? Why God treat us so? Man go work for donkey years then die like that? No enjoyment; no nothing; just suffer, suffer then die! How do I explain this to his relatives?"

"Missus, no blame God. Just tie heart – be strong. Look at the children; they are not crying much na? God will take care of them. They are strong; you go see."

"Mami Lucy, get up let's go prepare. Plenty of work dey ahead. This is not the time to be a woman; No be time this," Martin's neighbour advised Anastasia.

"Okay, Bessem. You be good woman. My Massa like you plenty. Okay."

She got up from the ground and hung on to Puis and Bessem until they arrived home. When she saw her children all crying and rolling on the ground in front of their house she burst out crying again and joined them there.

"You all will have to control yourself na?" Puis advised, extending one hand to pick each of them up from the ground. There was movement everywhere in the house as friends helped to pack up for the eventual trip to Martin's village. The factory blasted the time again and spewed dark smoke in the air. It toiled on churning more palm oil to be shipped somewhere including the one that would be used to cook enough food for Martin's funeral.

The company did not waste time. Everything was ready and just like Zacharias' situation there was a convoy waiting to escort Martin to his final resting place. As they left the place Martin had called home for almost forty years, it began to rain heavily. The ambulance driver chewed alligator pepper and told everyone to be ready. He poured kernel oil around the corpse to ward off evil spirits, then he grabbed a handful of masepo herbs, crushed these between his palms and rubbed all over his face. He was now ready to make the almost twenty-hour drive.

"Oya, let's go"

The wind grew fierce casting tree branches everywhere. Then lightning appeared and it began to thunder as the sky burst open in fury. Once the convoy was ready to drive away, the driver signalled John to pull out of the way so he could lead the delegation. John obeyed. The rain poured. The convoy drove slowly leaving the estate behind until they were a few meters away from the sign that said "Welcome to Lobe Estate: the one and only REAL PALM PLANTATION!" The lead driver honked a salute to Mr. Martin Tebi and edge away slowly driving past the sign and the boundary of the company property. He was almost out of that vicinity when the ambulance lost power and began stalling. The driver stopped and checked everything. There was nothing wrong with the engine of his vehicle. He hopped back in and turned the ignition key; the vehicle roared and stalled for a moment before losing power again. Unable to figure out what was the matter with the fairly new Land Rover that had been converted for use as the company ambulance, the driver requested that some of the men from the convoy push it and they did; but the vehicle that was about to transport Martin's remains refused to budge.

"Oya, everybody in," the driver ordered. He went round to the back and opened the coffin. "Now, Mr. Martin, you do as I say or else I will teach you something. Leave my imitation ambulance alone."

He closed the coffin and tried starting the vehicle again. It still would not start. He got out his whip and returned to the coffin. He whipped the coffin several times. "You see this whip, I carry for die people like you. You should have told your woman to bury you where you worked, since you like this place so much." He hit the coffin again. "Let me tell you something. I am a mere driver, so leave my motor alone. Next time na your skin proper ah go whip."

The others were shocked by the driver's behaviour. "What are you people looking at? Stubborn dead bodies must be handled with force. You people work so much and like the place so much that you don't want to go back. If you like Lobe too much, tell your people to respect that. No come humburg me!" He started his vehicle and it drove off. No one spoke as he drove away like a mad dog with his four wheel drive digging through the muddy road like nothing. They had not gone that far when a tree branch fell across the road. The driver stopped the vehicle and sighed. "Madam, this your man will give us trouble-oh?"

John walked over to see what was happening. In his heavy management raincoat he looked important. Martin would have liked that he was making an effort to do right by his daughter.

"Sir, it is tree this time that Mr. Martin has sent to come and punish us."

John nodded and returned to his car. The driver put on his own raincoat and went explaining to the different drivers how they would handle the situation. Soon they came up with a plan and chopped the tree off their path. The driver swore under his breath that whether Mr. Martin liked it or not, he was going back to where he had come from originally.

The more the rain poured the more slippery the road became. The men going to escort Martin dug their cars out of one ditch after another and pushed their way out of there until they hit the sections that were tarred and drove away like civilized people. When they returned from the trip the driver wrote a lengthy report and pleaded that they should transfer him to another department. He was tired of fighting with dead bodies that loved the company too much and did not want to go back to their real homes. His wish was granted and he thanked his God and like the others he forgot about Mr. Martin and his temper tantrums.

But Martin would not go in peace like everyone wanted. The harvesters said they saw his ghost in the bushes sitting still on his favourite rock. Bessem said she saw him playing draught on the veranda and talking to himself. All these stories caused panic on the estate and John had to supply every household with Manyanga. This kernel oil would help keep the troubled spirit away, he explained to the workers. Puis thought it was all rubbish. He knew his friend had died a happy man. He could tell from the way Martin had smiled the day he died knowing all the Big men were there to bid him farewell. So how could he be a ghost? If so, then he must be a happy ghost.

Epilogue

Six feet under the earth was not deep enough for Martin. He could still follow the clock as the company factory chimed time after time helping workers change shift, eat something, do something etc. The aroma of the freshly cooked palm fruits followed him down there keeping him from getting hungry. As he laid there in his dark solitary world he could not help but wonder if things had changed on the estate. "Not!" He would assure himself and adjust his body in the tiny box he now lived in. Above all, he could see things clearly now. He had made a choice he liked and could never forget the look on the faces of the people who surrounded his dead body on that fateful day, when it was his turn to depart. They liked him and wanted him to know that. He thought of Poor Puis now alone and who kept throwing excreta at people and thinking that no one knew. Of course, Martin had known all the time but what was the use telling anybody. Besides, had they all not gotten even with somebody on the estate? Even the Europeans too who pretended to be above God, had Zacharias not seen one tearing another's letter that had just arrived from overseas? Poor Zacharias to have died a hot death. He would give it to him; he died in excruciating pain but happy. He made a mental note to seek him out down there. Perhaps they could continue their draught game.

Martin reflected on his life so much that he soon found himself alive and actually sitting on his favourite rock enjoying the peace that the palm trees provided. He could hear the factory performing its humble duty and hoped the chimney was not sending something that may not be too nice in the air. He sighed and let it purr forever. Wasn't it doing its own best as well? Wasn't it?